Max Brand's
Best Western Stories
Volume II

Also available in Large Print
by Max Brand:

Trouble in Timberline
The Rangeland Avenger
Black Jack
The Blue Jay
Bull Hunter
Galloping Danger
The Gentle Gunman
Gunfighter's Return
Gunmen's Feud
The Making of a Gunman
The Man from the Wilderness
Rawhide Justice
Ride the Wild Trail
Rogue Mustang
Six-Gun Country
Storm on the Range
Three on the Trail
The Trail to San Triste
Wild Freedom

Max Brand's
Best Western Stories
Volume II

Edited with an Introduction by
William F. Nolan

G.K.HALL&CO.
Boston, Massachusetts
1986

The stories in this volume were originally published in the following magazines: *Star Western* ("Outcast," under the title "Outcast Breed"); *All-Story Weekly* ("The Fear of Morgan the Fearless"); *Country Gentleman* ("Dark Rosaleen"); *Western Story Magazine* ("Cayenne Charlie"); and *Liberty* ("The Golden Day").

Published in Large Print by arrangement with Dodd, Mead & Company, Inc.

British Commonwealth rights courtesy of Robert Hale Limited.

G. K. Hall Large Print Book Series.

Set in 18 pt Plantin.

Library of Congress Cataloging-in-Publication Data

Brand, Max, 1892–1944.
  Max Brand's best western stories.

  1. Western stories.   I. Nolan, William F., 1928–   .
II. Title.   III. Title: Best western stories.
[PS3511.A87A6   1986]   813'.52   86-4808
ISBN 0-8161-4011-1 (v. 2)

TO
Destry
　Dan Barry
　　The Montana Kid
　　　Jim Silver
　　　　Anthony Hamilton
　　　　Tizzo
　　　　　James Kildare

—*and to the memory of the man who gave them mythic life,*

FREDERICK SCHILLER FAUST

Contents

Acknowledgments

Once again, I am deeply indebted to Robert Easton, who arranged for the book's publication, supplied copies of all five stories, cleared permissions and aided in the selection of material. Mr. Easton's help is much appreciated; without him, this book would not exist.

My thanks, also, to Jane Faust Easton, to Brandt and Brandt and to the Estate of Frederick Faust.

W.F.N

Introduction

Success breeds success. This new compilation of Max Brand's best western tales is the direct result of a solid first volume, which was hailed by critics as "a worthy gathering of grand oldies" and "a strong and varied collection." *San Diego Magazine* called the stories "superb specimens of action and description," and the American Library Association's *Booklist* summed up *Max Brand's Best Western Stories* as "a fine anthology of the noted author's work."

A follow-up volume was obviously in order and, once again, I was asked to function as editor. I accepted with pleasure.

Frederick Faust, the legendary giant of popular fiction, wrote his westerns under a variety of pen names, the best known of which is Max Brand. (Western historian William Bloodworth called it "one of the most successful pseudonyms in the history of American publishing.") As Brand, he became "King of the Action Western," one of the few genuine masters of this genre.

How did he achieve such mastery? By the release of his "inner self." Fred Faust was a professional dreamer.

In one of his earliest stories, he wrote: "There are two selves in every man. The one self is that which others see—who walks the streets and labors and earns money and sweats and struggles under burdens . . . but there is another self—who accomplishes great deeds with consummate ease, who laughs at fear, who knows neither weariness nor self-doubt, who lives mightily, a strong, free, beautiful and terrible spirit. The wild desire to be that hidden self, to realize that personality in action, becomes the one worthwhile thing in life."

The exterior self Faust allowed the world to see was that of a hardheaded realist who often scorned his own best fiction—but the inner Faust was an idealist, a man of wildly romantic dreams, who lived in a world of heroic deeds and fabulous adventure that his extraordinary imagination kept constantly before him.

It is this unleashed spirit of romanticism that forms the heart of Max Brand's western tales.

In a recent study of popular fiction, Robert

Sampson analyzed Faust's unique talent: "His characters (both hero and villain) perform with really inhuman competence. Their abilities far exceed human physical limits. . . . They are figures belonging more to myth than to narrative fiction. . . . They materialize in prose glittering with detail, heated by emotion raised to poetic intensity. . . . The Brand stories exist at a singularly pure level, free of time's limits, in a world more open, more dangerous, more intense than our familiar present."

The world, in other words, of a professional dreamer.

Here in this book the dreamworld of Frederick Faust is brought to vivid life on each page. It is my sincere hope that this second collection of his best work in the western genre will inspire the publication of future volumes.

Max Brand's best stories release the dreamer in each of us as we enter the mythic western landscape of his wondrous imagination, sharing the wild escapades, the perilous pursuits and shootouts, the hairbreadth escapes.

The plains and mountains and valleys of Max Brand's West stretch before you; your horse is saddled and ready and a loaded Colt is at your hip; danger is waiting just beyond the horizon.

Let the adventure begin!

WILLIAM F. NOLAN
Agoura, California

Outcast

By 1934 Frederick Faust was into a major transitional phase of his career, as he moved from the fast-action pulp magazines into the higher-paying slick paper markets. That year saw top-quality Faust fiction printed in *Harper's* (under his real name), in *Collier's*, *Liberty* and *American Magazine*. His career as a western writer was drawing to a close. He would complete his final full-length pulp western late the following year, and would abandon western fiction entirely by the close of 1938.

However, despite the fact that he had been writing shoot-and-ride epics since 1917, his fictional resources were far from exhausted. Some of his best work in the western genre was printed during this transitional period. In fact, between early 1934 and the spring of 1935 he produced eight excellent Max Brand novelettes for *Star Western*. "Outcast" is perhaps the finest of the eight, delineating a theme often explored by Faust: the problems faced by a man of mixed blood fighting to sur-

1

vive prejudice and hostility in the Old West. During the course of his career Faust wrote many of these "white Indian" tales (from *Call of the Blood* to *The White Cheyenne*), and they are all a solid cut above the level of his more typical western fare.

With his sensitive portrait of John Cameron, the troubled hero of "Outcast," Faust achieves an ideal blend of action and character.

Here is Max Brand at his true best.

Cameron saw the ears of the rabbit above the rock when he was a hundred yards away. He began to stalk with the care he used to get at a deer; meat in even small portions was valuable to him and Mark Wayland. As long as the rifle ammunition held out they had fared well, but it is as hard to get within revolver-shot of desert game as it is to surprise a hawk in the naked sky.

Now, at his approach, three gray jackrabbits broke from the rock's shelter. Each ran in a different direction.

Cameron stood up as tall as his toes would lift him. The olive darkness of his face and the brown of his eyes lighted; he smiled a little; it was hard to tell whether cruelty or joy or a sort of pity inspired this smile. And then the revolver spoke to north, west, south, rapidly, the nose of it jerking at each explosion. The first two rabbits skidded along the earth, dead. His next shot accurately smashed the backbone of the third jackrabbit from end to end.

Before Cameron moved again, halted as he was in midstride, he rapidly reloaded the Colt in a single flowing gesture. Cameron picked up the game, cleaned it, and then stood straight once more to scan the horizon. A fox or a wolf will do this after the flurry of the

fight, when there is dead game to be eaten—
a last look towards all possible danger before
the feeding begins; and never a wolf had eyes
brighter than those of John Cameron.

It was during this rapid scanning of the
whole circle of the twilight that he saw the
glimmer on the head of the mountain, up
there on the height where stood his and Wayland's mine. That trembling gleam could be
but one thing—the shimmer of flame!

The shack was on fire. In some way—it was
inconceivable—Mark Wayland had permitted
the cabin to become ignited. Once the fire
caught on the wood—there was no water
available for the fight—there was nothing to
do but shovel earth at the flames. And perhaps the fire would spread into the shaft and
burn the timbers; the shaft would collapse;
the labor of the many months would be un-
done, just as they were sinking into the valuable heart of the vein, just as they were
writing the preface to a wealthy life, an easy
future divorced from sweat and worry.

Cameron, through the space needed for one
long breath, thought of these things. Then he
stripped the ragged shirt from his back,
wrapped the precious meat in it, and slinging
the shirt around his shoulders like a knapsack
he began to run.

He ran with his eye on the flame-spotted head of the mountain; as for the roughness of the terrain, his feet could see their own way. The half-Indian blood of his mother gave him that talent. Like an Indian, he toed in slightly, his body erect in spite of the weight on his back, his breathing deep and easy, an effortless spring in his stride. There was something of the deer about him, something of the predatory wild beast, also.

When he came to the end of the valley, he started up the ascent of the trailless slope with a shortened step. The weight of the rabbit meat was beginning to tell on him, now. The trembling exhaustion of effort, the agony of labor was stamped in the heaving of his lungs and in his shuddering belly-muscles; but it appeared only as a slight shadow on his face in the sweat that polished the bronze of his body.

So he came to the upper level, the head of the elevation where he and Mark Wayland had found the thin streak of color, long ago, and had begun their mine.

He had brighter light than that of the dusk, now. It came from the ruins of the cabin, weltering with flame. And out of the throat of the mine shaft issued a boiling mist of smoke.

The cabin was gone. The labor on the shaft was ruined also. Well, all of this could be reformed, redone. They had the plunder which many weeks of work in the heart of the vein had put into their hands—fifty pounds of gold dust, and perhaps it would be wiser anyway to take the money to town, turn part of it into hired labor, tools, powder, mules, and return to reopen the work with tenfold more advantage.

He thought of that as he stood on the edge of the little plateau and saw the flames.

But where was Mark Wayland? Where was that big, stocky body, that resolute face?

"Mark!" he shouted, "Mark!"

No answer. A dreadful surmise rushed into Cameron's mind, a sort of darkness, a storm across the soul.

He ran forward past the mouth of the mine, past the crumbling, flame-eaten timbers of the hoist, towards the fiery shambles of the cabin. Smouldering, charred logs lay here and there where they had rolled from the shack.

A more irregular shape was stretched on the ground.

He turned, leaned over the body of Mark Wayland.

Strong wires had been twisted around the arms, fastening them helplessly to the sides. The legs had been wired together at the knees and also at the ankles. There was a gag

6

crammed into the mouth, distending it wide. Fire had eaten the body.

Someone had caught Mark by surprise, robbed the cabin, bound Wayland, and trusted to the fire to rub out the record of the crime. And then Cameron saw that the eyes of the dead man were living.

A cry came from Cameron like the scream of a bird. He snatched the gag from Wayland's mouth, severed the wires that bound him, then picked up the great, smoking hulk of the body in his arms to carry it to the life-giving waters of the creek.

The voice of Wayland stopped him. The voice was calm. "I'm dead," said he. "I'm already in hell, John. There's nothing to do for me now."

Cameron eased Wayland to the ground. With bare hands he stopped the red coals of fire that ate at the clothes of the victim.

"A gray mustang," gasped Wayland. "He was riding a gray mustang with a lopped ear—lopped left ear. A big sort of man . . . Give me your gun!"

"No, Mark!" shouted Cameron. "I'll take care of you. I'll make you well!"

"God!" gritted Wayland. "Don't you see that I'm burned to the bone?"

"Mark, for God's sake, let me try and—"

"Are you gonna show yourself a damn weakling?" groaned Wayland. A shudder of pain passed through him. "John . . . I *need* your gun!"

Slowly, Cameron drew his big Colt revolver and dropped it on the ground. He whirled, and began to run. But he realized that he could not run beyond the sound of the gunshot and cast himself down on his face, with his hands clasped over his ears.

But he heard, nevertheless. It seemed as though the noise were conducted to him through the earth. His body drank it in not through the ears only but through every nerve. It was a deep, short, hollow, barking noise. And it meant that Mark Wayland was dead.

The whole future was snatched away from Cameron; the whole chance of making a return to his benefactor. And all the love that he had poured out towards Wayland was blown away with that shot.

But there was one thing to live for. There was the man—the big sort of man, who rode a gray mustang with a lopped left ear. Cameron got up from the earth as a cat rises from sleep at the scent of prey.

The trail could not be followed by night.

Cameron spent the darkness in digging a grave. He carried to the grave the dead man with the flame-eaten body and the purple-rimmed hole in the right forehead. Into the pit he lowered the dead man. Over the body he first laid with his hollowed hands a layer of brush, because he could not endure the thought of rocks and earth pressing on the dead face.

Afterwards, he took the revolver and went on the trail.

He followed the trail across the desert. It took him three days to get to the hills and to the town of Gallop. There the sign disappeared.

The only description he had of the rider was of a "big sort of man," and Gallop was filled with big men. Therefore, he left the town and cut for the sign and circled around the town. Every day he made the circuit until at last, on the old desert trail, he found what he was looking for. He had not been able to spot the gray horse in Gallop, but he had found the trail of it leading from the place.

For two days, the flesh melted from the body of John Cameron as he struggled along the traces of the trail.

At the end of the second day, he saw a winking fire in a patch of mesquite beside an

9

alkali water-hole. Standing nearby, eating from a nosebag, was a gray mustang with a Roman nose—a dirty-gray mustang with a yellow stain in the unspotted portion of its hide. Its left ear was lopped off an inch from the point.

By the fire sat a big man with a broad, red face and red hair. When Cameron looked at him, he smiled, and took a deep breath. The weariness of running slipped from his body. The tremor of exhaustion passed from his nerves. His hands became quiet and sure.

He stood at the edge of the firelight. "Put up your hands," said Cameron.

The red-faced man shook his head.

"You won't get anything off me except a hoss and a half a side of bacon, brother," he said.

"Stand up!" commanded Cameron.

The red-faced man grunted. "Aw—well—" he said. And he rose to his feet.

"You've got a gun on your hip," said Cameron. "Use it!"

"What's the matter?" shouted the other. "My God, you ain't gonna murder me, *are* you?"

Fear rounded his eyes. He looked like a pig, soggy with fat for the market. A horror surged up in Cameron when he thought that this was the man who had killed Mark Wayland. As well conceive of a grizzly slain by a swine.

"Look!" said Cameron. "I'll give you a fair chance. I'm putting my gun up and we'll take an even start—"

He holstered his big Colt. And, instantly, the man who looked like a pig snatched his own gun out, suddenly, and started fanning it at Cameron with the flick of a very expert thumb. He should have crashed at least one bullet through the brain of John Cameron except that Cameron's instinct was as keen as a wolf. It told his feet what to do and as he side-stepped, the Colt was again in his hand.

If he could kill three scattering rabbits on the run he could kill one red-faced swine that was standing still. Cameron drove a bullet for the middle of the breast. It changed on metal instead of thudding against flesh. The revolver, jerked out of the fat fingers, was hurled back into the red face, knocking the big man to the ground.

"Pick up your gun and we'll start again," said Cameron tightly.

The other pushed himself up on his hands. There was a bump rising on his forehead but otherwise he had not been hurt. "Who are you?"

"My name is Cameron. Stand up!"

"I ain't gonna stand up. God Almighty saved my life once tonight, but he won't save it twice. Cameron, I never done you harm. Why are you after me?"

"You've done me more harm than any man can ever do!" exclaimed Cameron. He came a little closer, drawn by his anger. Hatred pulled the skin of his face taut. "When you did your murder—when you wired him into a bundle and left him to burn in the cabin— you didn't know that he'd manage to crawl out of the fire and live long enough to put me on your trail. But—"

"Wired into a bundle—burn in the cabin— what are you talking about, Cameron? I never killed a man in my life!"

"What's your name?"

"Jess Cary."

"Where did you get the gray horse?"

"From Terry Wilson, back there in Gallop."

"What sort of looking man is Wilson?"

"Big sort of feller."

Surety that he was hearing the truth struck home in the brain of Cameron. He began to tremble. It was as though God had indeed turned the bullet from the heart of Jess Cary; and only for that reason were the hands of

Cameron clean.

He had a last glimpse of Jess Cary glowering hopelessly after him from the small, ragged circle of the firelight. Then he turned and struck back through the night.

When he reached a run of water in the hills at the edge of the desert, he stopped the swinging dogtrot with which he covered ground and lay down to rest. Infinite fatigue made the earth a soft bed. As for the hunger which consumed him, a notch taken up in his belt quieted that appetite. In a moment he was asleep.

He had five hours of rest by dawn. Fatigue still clouded his brain, so he stripped, swam in a pool of the stream, whipped the water from his brown body, dressed and ran on toward Gallop with the same effortless pace which drifted him over the trail. A jackrabbit rose from nothingness and dissolved itself with speed. He tipped it over with a snap shot and ate half-roasted meat, sitting on his heels at a hot, smokeless fire of dry twigs.

That night he slept three more hours, ran on again, and entered Gallop in the early morning when life was beginning to stir. He had two bullets left in his gun, but two would be enough.

The blacksmith had the doors of his shop open and was starting a fire in his forge. "Terry Wilson—can you tell me where I can find him?" asked Cameron.

The blacksmith looked up from the gloom of the shop.

"Wilson. Sure. He's got the corral at the end of the town. He's the horse-dealer."

The horse-dealer! Lightness went out of the step of Cameron, as he turned away. He had thought that vengeance was about to fill his hand. Instead, it was probable that Wilson was only another milestone pointing down the trail of the manhunt.

He reached the corrals in time to see a new herd driven through the gates of the largest enclosure. They washed around the lofty fences like water around the lip of a bowl. Dust rose in columns, a signal smoke against the sky. Dust spilled outwards in billows, and in that mist Cameron found a big fellow who was pointed out to him.

"Mr. Wilson," he said, "you sold a lop-eared gray to Jess Cary, didn't you?"

The man turned his eye from the contemplation of the horses.

"Jess stick you with that no-account mustang?"

14

"Where did you buy the gray?" asked Cameron.

"Tierney," answered Terry Wilson. "Will Tierney." His eye changed as he stared at Cameron. "Ain't you Mark Wayland's breed?" he demanded.

The question stiffened the spine of Cameron. He had to force himself to turn on his heel, slowly, and walk away.

It was not the first time he had heard the word. Breed, usually, or half-breed in full, slurring from men with no friendliness for any part of Cameron's heritage. Was it always to strike at him like poison in his shadow? And why? He could wish that he had not led such a secluded life with Mark Wayland. He knew something of grammar and books; he knew the wilderness; but he knew nothing of men.

His mother's mother had been a beauty of the Blackfoot tribe, a queen of her kind. Was there not honor in such blood? And a chieftain of the frontier had married her. Was not their daughter able to hold up her head even before thrones?

Three parts of his blood were white, and as for the other part, he could see in it nothing but glory. Yet the world called him breed as it might have called him cur!

He learned that Will Tierney would be

leaving the hotel at noon. Very well. Cameron would wait for him.

He found a tree in the little plaza opposite the hotel and sat on his heels to smoke a cigarette and think. Sun was filling the world. Over the roof of the hotel he could look up the gorge of Champion Creek and see the bright dazzle of cliffs on its western side. There was beauty and peace to be found; but where white men moved in numbers there was insult, cruelty—

The morning wore away. The sun climbed. The heat increased. A magnificent fellow came down the steps of the hotel and strode along the street. There was a flash and a glory about him. He had that distinction of face which is recognized even at a distance. He bore himself with the pride of a champion. And if his blue silk shirt and silver conchos down his trousers and glint of Mexican wheelwork around his sombrero made a rather gaudy effect, it would be forgiven as the sheen of a real splendor of nature.

So this was Will Tierney? Cameron could have wished the name on a fellow of a different aspect, but nevertheless he would have to accost the handsome giant. He was up and after him instantly, and followed him through the swing-doors of Grady's Saloon

16

on the corner.

Inside, at the bar, Cameron stepped to the shoulder of Tierney and said: "You sold a lop-eared gray mustang to Terry Wilson. Do you mind telling me where you got the horse?"

Tierney's upper lip pulled back in a sneer that showed his teeth. His eyes were the black of a night that is polished by stars. He nodded to the bartender.

"Grady," he said, "since when have you been letting breeds drink in your place?"

The bartender grunted. "Is that a breed? By God, it is! *Out* of here! Get out of my place!"

A hard-muscled cowpuncher with a bull-dog face shook a fist at Cameron.

"That means *you!*" he growled.

Tierney stood back against the bar with one hand on his hip, the other dangling close to the butt of a revolver that was strapped to his thigh. He was laughing.

"You—Tierney—it's *you* that I want to talk to!" exclaimed Cameron. "Where did you get that gray horse?"

The cowpuncher with the face of a bulldog drove a big fist straight at the head of Cameron. His punch smote thin air as Cameron dodged—right into the sway of another powerful blow. There were a dozen enemies, all bearing down. He tried to shift through them. Hands caught at him. Fingers groped into his writhing flesh. His gun was snatched away. A swinging Colt clipped the side of his head and half-stunned him.

Then he was through the swinging doors. The sunlight along the street was like a river of white fire that flowed into his bewildered brain. Hands thrust him forward. He was kicked brutally from behind and pitched on face and hands into the burning dust of the street.

"Where's a whip?" called the clear, ringing voice of Tierney. "We'll put a whip to this dog!"

A whiplash cut across the back of Cameron and brought him swiftly to his feet in time to take another lash across his shoulder and breast. Then a rider plunged between him and the Grady crowd.

The horse skidded to a halt; a girl's voice shouted: "What a crew of cowards you are! A dozen of you on one man! Will Tierney, isn't there any shame in you? Jack—Tom Culbert—Harry—I'll remember that you were all in this!"

They scattered before her words as before bullets. Two or three hurried down the street; the rest streamed back through the swing-doors of Grady's saloon. Their shouted laughter beat on the brain of Cameron.

He looked up into the gray eyes and the brown, serious face of the girl. She wore a blouse of faded khaki, a well-battered divided riding skirt of the same stuff. But every inch of the horse she rode spoke of money. That was not what mattered. The thing she had done talked big in the mind of Cameron. And it seemed to him that he could look into the beauty of her face as far and as deep as into the loveliness of a summer evening.

"It was rotten of them!" the girl flared. "I don't care what you were doing—it's rotten for a dozen to pick on one men."

He put his hand over his shoulder and tentatively felt the welts which the whiplash had left. They were still burning.

"I'm Jacqueline Peyton. Who are you?"

"John Cameron."

"You look hungry," she said, "and those cuts need tending. I live near town. Will you come along with me?"

"I could use a meal," admitted Cameron.

She dismounted, began walking beside him.

"You can ride," he said.

"I don't ride when a friend is walking," she said firmly.

He walked beside her down the middle of the street.

"What are you doing in town, John?"

"Looking for a man—and I think I've found him."

"Is that good news or bad news for him?"

"I have to kill him," said Cameron slowly.

She looked pale. *"Why,* John?"

"Because he murdered my friend," said Cameron.

"But there's the *law*. You can't—"

He lifted his hands and looked down at them curiously.

"If the law hanged him, there would be nothing to fill my hands; there would be no feeling—there would be no taste," said Cameron, gently.

She stared at him.

"He was tied with wire and left in a burning cabin," said Cameron. "And I came back before he was dead. He lived long enough to tell me what sort of horse the murderer rode. He told me that and he asked me for my gun. Then he killed himself."

"No!" cried the girl. "It isn't possible that you let him kill himself!"

"He was burned," said Cameron, "until his face was loose with cooking. It was ready to rub away. He was burned like a roast on a spit. That was why I gave him the gun. Before he had to begin screaming with pain."

The girl lowered her head in shock.

"I've never heard of anything so terrible. It makes me want to help you. How *can* I help you, John?"

"By letting me walk up the road with you."

"Walk up the road?" she repeated, bewildered.

He felt his face grow hot. He swallowed, and said after a moment of silence: "I haven't seen very much of people, and I don't know how to talk." He walked on beside her. "But this is a happiness for me. Just being able to walk here with you."

At the moment they passed the top of the hill and saw a string of a dozen or more Indians riding across the main trail; they crossed into the trees and were gone.

"They're heading up toward the new reservation," said the girl.

Something stirred in the heart of John Cameron, and he looked earnestly after the vanished file of riders. But now a turn of the trail brought them to the Peyton ranch, suddenly, the confusion of the big corrals, a grove of cottonwoods and the low, broad forehead of the house itself showing over the rim of the rise.

Her father would be inside, she said. She gave her mare to a boy who loitered near the hitching rack and took Cameron straight into the house.

The living room was a big, barnlike hall where a dance or a meeting could have been held. Over in a corner, in a leather chair, sprawled a man with gray hair and a grayish care-worn face. He looked up from the papers spread out before him and rumbled: "Well, and who have you brought home?"

"John Cameron," said the girl. "He needs a good meal—and a bit of mending. He was cut up in town."

"How?" asked Peyton. "What happened?"

Before a reply could be given, hoofbeats swept up to the front of the house, and three big men entered the room. One of them was Will Tierney.

He glared at Cameron. "What's the idea, bringing a breed home, Jackie?"

"I don't know what you—" began the girl.

"Breed!" growled Peyton. He squinted at John Cameron.

Tierney stepped closer. "The gall of him, coming here. He'll regret it!"

Cameron looked not at all at this approaching danger. He considered the girl only, and saw her eyes widen with confusion.

Then he turned toward Will Tierney and the others.

The two tall, fair-haired men had something of the look of Jacqueline about them. They were her brothers, surely.

"Kick him out of here!" cried one, and he struck Cameron across the mouth with the flat of his hand. Then they swept Cameron to the door and hurled him through it.

The wind was at the back of John Cameron, helping him, and it was still early night when he came again into the long, winding main street of Gallop. Fire still burned in the forge of the blacksmith; he was still hammering at his anvil when the voice at his door made him look up and see the same agile, light form he had noticed that morning.

"I need your help again," said Cameron. "Where can I find Les Harmody?"

"At the ole Decker place, straight on down the street. Half-mile maybe."

Cameron found the place easily. His mind was weighted by the sense of duty. He had to find Will Tierney and make sure that Tierney was indeed the murderer of Wayland.

Les Harmody might be the man to help. Mark had spoken often of Harmody; they had once been close friends.

Cameron tapped with a reverent hand at the door of the shack. A faint light seeped through the cracks in the flimsy wall.

"Come in!" thundered a great voice.

He pulled the door open and stepped inside. The wind slammed the door shut behind him because what he saw loosened the strength of his fingers. He never had seen such a man; he never had hoped to see one.

Somewhere between youth and grayness, young enough to retain speed of hand and old enough to have his strength hardened upon him, Les Harmody filled the mind and the eye.

The shaggy forelock and the weight of the jaw gave a certain brutality to his face but the enormous power that clothed his shoulders and his arms was the main thing. His wrist was as round and as hard as an apple, filled with compacted sinews of power and the iron bone of strength underneath.

He was eating a thick steak with a mug of coffee placed beside it. Gristle crackled between his teeth.

"Are you Les Harmody?" asked Cameron.

"And what if I am?" growled the big man.

"I need your help."

"I don't help breeds! Get out!"

Cameron stiffened, eyes hard. "You're

treating me no better than a dog."

"All breeds is dogs," said Harmody.

"Dogs have teeth," answered Cameron, and stepping still closer, he leaned and flicked his hand across the face of the giant.

Harmody's eyes measured Cameron and the distance to the door which assured him that the victim could not escape. He leaned one great hand on the table and in the other raised the mug of coffee, which he emptied at a draught. He wiped his dripping lips on the back of his hand as he put down the cup.

"I'll have decent talk from you," said Cameron. "I'll have it—if I have to tear it out of your throat!"

Harmody did not walk around the table. He brushed it aside with a light gesture and all the dishes on it made a clattering.

"You'll tear it out of me?" he said softly, and then he lunged for Cameron.

Up there in the mountain camps, patiently, with fists bare, Mark Wayland had taught his foster son something of the white man's art of self-defense. Cameron used the lessons now. He had no hope of winning; he only hoped that he might prove himself a man.

Speed of foot shifted him aside from the first rush. He hit Harmody three times on the side of the jaw as the big target rushed past.

It was like hitting a great timber with sacking wrapped over it.

Harmody stopped his rush, turned. He pulled a gun and tossed it aside. "I'm gonna kill you," he said through his teeth, "but I don't want tools to do the job! A breed—a damned, lousy breed—to make a fool out of me, eh?"

He came again, not blindly, but head up, balanced inside himself, as a man who understands boxing. Even if he had been totally ignorant, to stand up to him would have been like standing up to a grizzly. But he had skill to back his power. He was fast, bewilderingly fast for a man of his poundage.

He feinted with a left. He repeated with the same hand, and the blow grazed the head of Cameron. It was as though the hoof of a brass-shod stallion had glanced from his skull. The weight of the blow flung him back against the wall and Harmody rushed in to grasp his helpless victim.

But Harmody's arms reached for nothingness. Cameron had slid away with a ducking sidestep. He had to look on his own fists as tack hammers. They would avail only if they hit the right place a thousand times, breaking down the nerve centers with repeated shocks.

Swift blows thudded on the jaw of Harmody, as he swayed around. He tried the left feint and repeat. Again, the blow was side-stepped.

Wings were under the feet of Cameron. If only there were more room than this shack afforded—if only he had space to maneuver in, then he could swoop and retreat and swoop again until he had beaten this monster into submission. But he had to keep constant thought of the walls, the overturned chairs, the table which had crashed on its side and extended its legs to trip him. One slip, one fall, would be the end of him.

Yet, with every passing moment, he was growing more sure, more steady. He changed from the jaw and shot both hands for the wind. His right thumped on the ribs as on the huge round of a barrel, and the left dug deep into the rubbery stomach muscles. Harmody grunted.

And then he reached Harmody's glaring eyes with hooking punches that jarred back the massive head. He reached the wide mouth and puffed and cut the lips. They fought silently, except for the noise of their gasping breath.

And always there was the terrible danger that one of Harmody's massive punches would strike home. Then the devil that was lodged behind his eyes would have its chance at full expression.

A glancing blow laid open the cheek of Cameron. He felt the hot run of blood down his face.

But that was nothing. Nothing compared with the stake for which he fought. Not merely to endure for a time, but actually to win, to conquer, to beat this great hulk into submission!

He fought for that. He never struck in vain. For the eyes, for the mouth, for the vulnerable side of the chin, or for the soft of the belly—those were his targets.

A hammer-stroke brushed across his mouth—merely brushed across it—but slashed the lips open and brought a fresh down-pouring of blood. In return, he stepped aside and tattooed the body and then the jaw of Harmody.

The big fellow was no longer an exhaustless well of energy. He paused between rushes. His mouth opened wide to take greater breath. Sweat dripped down his face and mingled with the blood. But the flaming devil in his eyes was still bright.

Exhaustion began to work in Cameron, also. He had to run, to dance, to keep himself poised as on wings. Preliminary tremors of weakness began to run through his body. He saw that he would have to bring it to an end—meet one of those headlong charges and literally knock the monster away from him. It was impossible—but it was the only way.

He saw the rush start and he moved as though to leap to either side. Instead, he sprang in, ducked the driving first that tried to catch him, and hammered a long overhand right straight against the jaw of Harmody.

The solid shock, his running weight and lashing blow against the rush of Harmody, turned his arm numb to the shoulder.

But Les Harmody was stopped. He was halted, he was put back on his heels, he was making little short steps to the rear, to regain his balance!

Cameron followed like a greedy wildcat. The right hand had no wits in it, now. He used the left, then, and with three full drives he found the chin of Les Harmody.

He saw the great knees buckle. The head and shoulders swayed. The guarding, massive arms dropped first, and then Harmody sank to the floor.

Cameron stepped back. He wanted to run in and crash his fist home behind the ear—a stroke that would end the fight. But there were rules in this game and a fallen man must not be hit.

So Cameron stood back, groaning with eagerness, and saw the loosened hulk on its knees and on one supporting hand.

"Have you had enough?" gasped Cameron.

"Me?" groaned Les Harmody. "Me? Enough? Damn your rotten heart—"

He lurched to his feet. Indignation seemed to burn the darkness out of his brain, and again he charged forward.

Once more, Cameron stepped in to check the rush. This time his fist flew high—his right shoulder was still aching from the first knockdown—and he felt the soggy impact against the enormous head.

It was a hard blow, but it was not enough to stop Harmody. A great fist loomed before the eyes of Cameron. He tried to jerk away from its path, but it shot upward too swiftly. The shock seemed not under the jaw but at the back of his brain. He fell forward.

Consciousness came back to him after that, in lurid flashes. He was dead. It was his ghost, wakening in another world.

Then Cameron was aware of lights around him, and the wide flash of a mirror's face. There were exclaiming voices. There was a greater voice than all others, the thunder of

Les Harmody. A mighty hand upheld him, wavering. A powerful shoulder braced against him.

Cameron saw his own face, dripping crimson, swollen, purple here and running blood there. He saw the face of Les Harmody beside his own—and the big man's features had been battered out of shape, a ghastly mass of bruised, hammered flesh.

This monster was shouting, out of a swollen mouth: "Here's the fellow who stood up to me—me—Les Harmody! By God, I thought that the time would never come when I'd have the pleasure of standin' hand to hand with any *one* man. Look at him, you coyotes, you sneakin' house dogs that run and yammer when a wolf comes to town! Look at him— here's plenty of wolf for you! Look at the skinny size of him who fought Les Harmody man to man, and knocked me down. And then, by God, he stood back and gave me my chance to stand *again!*"

Harmody dipped his bandanna into a schooner of beer, drew it out, sopping, crushed the excess liquid from it, and then carefully sponged the bleeding face of Cameron.

The cold sting of the beer helped to rouse him completely.

"Speak up,—d'you see him?" thundered Harmody. "Grady, you fat-faced buzzard, d'you see him now?"

"I see him, Les."

"Then, I ask you, is he a good man, damn you?"

"That he is, Les."

"I'll warn the lot of you—any man that calls him a breed again will have me to reckon with."

He turned to Cameron. "Listen, kid—are you feelin' better? I wanted them to see you, and what you done to me. I wanted the whole damn world to see. Kid, will you drink with me? Can you stand, and can you drink? Whisky, Grady. Damn you, move fast. Whisky for the kid. Here I've been searching the world for a gent with the nerve and the hands to stand up to me. Here's to the man that done it. Every one of you drink to him. Bottoms up!" And they drank.

There was music in the Peyton house. Joe Peyton thrummed a banjo; Harry and Will Tierney sang while Oliver Peyton composed himself in a deep chair with his hands folded behind his head, a contented audience. They had not heard the pounding hoofs of a big horse approach the house, but they were aware of the creaking of the floor in the hall as someone walked toward them, and now the great figure that loomed in the doorway silenced the song. Oliver Peyton rose to his feet.

"Hey, Les Harmody!" he called. "I'm glad to see you, old son. Come in and sit down. What will you be drinking?"

Harmody accepted the extended hand rather gingerly.

"Thanks," he said. "But I'm not here for drinking. And for what I've got to say I reckon that standing will be best."

"What's the matter, Les?" asked Oliver Peyton, frowning anxiously. "You talk as though you had a grudge, old-timer?"

"By a way of speaking I ain't got a grudge," said Harmody. "But in another way, I got a pretty deep one. I've come from a friend, and a better friend no man ever had. You know John Cameron?"

"The breed?" asked Tierney.

Harmody started. "That's the wrong word for him, Will. I've stood up and told people that 'breed' ain't the word for him. But maybe you weren't around when I did my talking. His grandmother was a Blackfoot that could of married a chief. There's proud blood in him, understand?"

"Blood is blood," said Will Tierney. "And

he's a breed, to me."

Harmody took in a big breath. "We'll find a better place to argue it out, one day."

"Any place, any time would be fine," said Tierney, and his bright eyes measured Harmody steadily.

"Stop it, Will!" commanded Oliver Peyton. "It only riles Les. Can't you see that? Les, I wish you'd sit down!"

"I'll say it standing," answered Harmody. "I've been away in the hills for pretty near a month with Cameron. It takes time to learn to know a friend but I've learned to know him. On a horse, or on his feet, with his hands or with a gun, I never found a better man. But he's got ideas."

He paused, when he said this, and ran his eyes over the group.

"I've done a lot of talking and reasoning with him," went on Harmody, "but the main thing is that he feels he's given his word, and he's given it to God Almighty. So he'll keep it! He means to kill, and nothing's going to stop the killin'."

This struck silence across the room.

Harmody went on: "You're the one, Tierney, and he wants to have the death of you because of what you done to Mark Wayland. And if he's right, I'd like to do the job on you myself!"

"He's crazy!" said Tierney.

Harmody went on: "He says there was around fifty pounds in gold dust. And he points out that inside the last ten days you've made a payment on the land where you're going to live with Jacqueline. You made that payment with thirty pounds of gold dust."

"Will!" cried the girl.

She'd just entered the room, and was now staring at Tierney.

"You stay out of this, Jackie," snapped Will Tierney.

Harmody backed to the door.

"I come in here being sorry I had to bring bad news," he said. "But the longer I've stayed here, the more I've felt the kid is right, Tierney. And if you done that job, God help your soul!"

Then he was gone through the doorway.

Behind him, Tierney was saying: "Something has to be done about this. A skunk like that breed poisoning the air with his lies—"

"Will," said the girl, "*is* it a lie?"

He spun about to confront her white face.

"Jackie, are you *believing* him?" he shouted.

She stared at him for a moment. "I don't know. I don't know what to believe, except that John Cameron is an honest man!"

And she left the room.

In the corral she caught up her favorite mare and was quickly on the road. She turned in the saddle with a desperate eagerness, scanning the horizon, and so made out, very dimly, the movement of a shape over a hill and against the horizon.

She struck out in that direction.

It was the eastern trail and she flew the mare along it for half a mile. Then she slowed to a walk and heard distinctly, out of the distance, the clacking of hoofs over a stretch of stony ground.

"Les!" she began to cry aloud. "Les Harmody!"

A deep-throated shout answered her at once; she saw the huge man and the horse looming against the stars on the next hummock.

"That you, Jacqueline? What's wrong?"

"I want to go with you—to see John, to beg him to leave. They'll *kill* him, Les!"

"It's no use," said Harmody. "He won't go."

"I want to try, through. I *have* to try to persuade him."

"D'you like Cameron?"

"I like him a lot."

"Come along, then. A woman can sometimes do what a man can't manage. I've begged him hard to give up this job. He's been like a stone, though."

They rode on together, leaving the trail presently and plunging into a thicket of brush higher than their heads. Finally, through the dark mist of brush, she could see the pale gleam of a light that showed them into a small clearing where the ruins of a squatter's shack leaned feebly to the side, ready to fall. By the fire Cameron answered the call of Harmody.

"Who's coming with you?" he snapped. "What made you—" He broke off when he saw the girl. He looked older, now. Across one cheekbone was the jagged red of a new scar which time, perhaps, would gradually dim.

She went straight up to him when she had dismounted and offered her hand.

"The last time, at the house, when they said all those awful things to you, I insulted you by keeping silent when I should have spoken up. Can you forgive, John?"

He took her hand. His grave eyes studied her face. "They told you the truth," he said. "I *am* a half-breed."

She shook her head, dismissing his words.

"I'm beginning to realize what a *man* you are. I guessed it when we walked up that road together. I knew it when I heard what you'd done to Les Harmody. It's because I know what a man you are that I've come here tonight."

"Les should never have brought you."

"She follered me, John," protested Harmody. "What was I to do? And besides, I thought she might show you the best way out of this whole mess."

"That's it, of course," said Cameron, gloomily. "I have to be persuaded. But there's no good in that, Jacqueline. No good at all. I've given a promise I'll have to keep."

She was silent.

"You see how it is?" said the grumbling voice of Harmody. "Nothing can budge him."

"There's only one thing I wish," said Cameron, "that none of this meant anything to you. . . . But Tierney—I know you're going to marry him—"

"He's nothing to me!"

"He has to be. You're marrying him!" exclaimed Cameron.

"I give you my word and my honor, he's nothing to me, now. Because I think—I really think—he did the frightful thing you told me about."

"You're through with him?"

"Yes. I never really loved him. It was simply growing up together, and going riding and dancing together, and being encouraged by everyone."

"Sit down here, Jacqueline. Here by the fire. That's better. I can see your eyes now. Just *looking* at you, my heart stirs."

"Hold up now," said Les Harmody. "You can't talk to a girl like that!"

"Can't I?" asked Cameron, startled. "Have I said something wrong?"

"Not a word!" said the girl.

"All he knows is hunting and reading," said Harmody. "He don't know nothing about people. You can't let him talk to you like that."

"Why not? I like it."

"But doggone it, Jacqueline, unless he loves you—"

"I do," said Cameron. "Does that make it all right?"

Les Harmody stared at him. "What's the matter with you? You've only met her once before!"

"True," said Cameron. "But that meeting brought me more happiness in a few minutes than all the rest of my life put together."

The girl smiled up at Harmody. "You may

know a lot about women, Les," she said, "but John Cameron happens to know a lot about me."

She put out a hand and touched the arm of Cameron.

"That's why I've had the courage to come up here tonight. It *can't* go on! John, you can't take the blood-trail against Tierney! Leave him to the law. There *is* a law for that sort of a man!"

"If you'd been raised by Wayland and then found him dying as I found him—wouldn't you despise yourself if you waited for the law to do your work on the murderer?"

But before she could answer, the voice of Will Tierney barked from the edge of the brush: "Stick up your hands! Fast!"

"What in hell—" began Harmody.

"You're out of this, Les!" shouted the voice of Joe Peyton. "Stand aside."

Cameron had risen to his feet. The girl threw herself in front of him.

"Don't shoot!" she screamed. "Will, don't shoot him!"

Will Tierney came out from the brush at a gliding pace, his feet touching the earth softly for fear that he might upset his aim, the revolver held well out before his body.

"Get away from him!" he shouted. "Step

away or I'll get him *through* you, by God!"

Cameron had waited for a single second, stunned. Now he turned and dived for the brush. He ran as a snipe flies, dodging rapidly from side to side and yelling: "Harmody, it's my fight. Stay out of it!"

He heard the scream of the girl, then the guns began. Bullets whistled past his head; the brush crashed before his face. He was instantly in the thick gloom of the foliage, safe for that moment. Then he heard the shrill cry of the girl: "Will! You've shot Les Harmody!"

The words struck him to a halt. He stood gripping at the trunk of a sapling until the palm of his hand ached, and behind him he heard Harmody's deep, broken voice exclaiming: "I'm all right, Jacqueline. Don't worry about me. I'm all right. But I tell the rest of you for your own good—don't go into that brush after Cameron. If you go in there, he'll kill you as sure as God made wildcats! He ain't got a gun! But he's got hands that are almost as good as a gun."

They did not press into the brush, but Will Tierney exclaimed: "It's the breed that ought to be lying here, not Harmody. Les, it's your own fault! If you hadn't got between me and my aim, I'd have Cameron dead as a bone. He dodged—damn him, he dodged like a bird in the air! I never saw such a thing!"

"You never saw such a man-eater, either," declared Harmody. "And he'll chaw your bones one day, Tierney."

"Stop all this talk!" commanded the girl. "Help me carry him into the shack, Joe— Harry, take his shoulders. Gently, boys."

From the brush, Cameron watched the men carrying big Les Harmody through the open door of the shack. Will Tierney, coming back into the clearing, kicked some more wood onto the fire and made the flames jump. This brighter light seemed to be a comfort to him. He walked in an uneasy circle around the fire, staring toward the brush.

Inside the cabin they were examining the wound of Harmody. Once he groaned aloud as though under a searching probe. Then the girl was saying: "He needs a doctor. I'll stay here with him. The rest of you go straight for town."

Tierney stepped to the door of the shack. "I'd like nothing better than to tackle Cameron—but he's run away."

"I think you like murder better'n you like fighting," said Les Harmody.

"When you're on your feet," answered Tierney, "I'll give you your chance at me, any time!"

"I'll take you up on that one day," said Harmody.

The girl was glaring at Tierney. "I saw it! You fired to kill!"

"The fool was in my path," said Tierney. "What else was I to do? He came between me and Cameron."

"Get out of my sight!" said Jacqueline. "I never want to see your face again!"

Tierney strode into the shack, shouting something that was lost to the straining ears of Cameron, because all the men were speaking at once.

Then, through a pause, Cameron could hear Tierney crying out: "You prefer a breed, maybe?"

"I prefer John Cameron and I don't care what you call him!" she answered. "Now, all of you—go get Doc Travis. *Now!*"

The three men came striding out of the shack.

"It's no good," Tierney was saying. "You can see she's been hypnotized by that rat Cameron. I'm going to have the killing of him."

They went away across the clearing, hastily, and as the brush closed after them, there was a great impulse in Cameron to run forward to the shack and show himself for one instant to the girl he loved, and to Les Harmody who with his own body had stopped the bullets that were intended for him.

But there was something more for Cameron to do than to speak to the woman he loved or to touch the hand of his friend. He had to strike down Tierney. If God would let him, he had to strike at Will Tierney now. He was on foot, he was weaponless, and there were three men against him, two of whom were sacred from any serious injury at his hands. They were Jacqueline's brothers, and that fact would save their lives. But he must act now.

Cameron knew Tierney would probably get out of the country as fast as possible. He had lost his chance at a rich marriage; there now hung over his head the accusation of murder; Will Tierney would ride with the Peytons, go as far as Gallop, deliver the message to the doctor, and then slip away for good. There would be no time to catch him, therefore, except this night. And already the horses of the three were galloping steadily away.

The riders would have to wind down through the hills to come to the head of the steep-walled Long Chance Ravine. For his own part, Cameron could strike straight across country.

As he ran, John Cameron snatched off his

shirt, tore it into strips, and began to knot the tough strips together. He left the woods, slipped through a pass between two hills, and so found himself at the Long Chance. It ran straight east towards Gallop, bordered with cliffs to the north and south, sheer faces of rock.

On the level floor of the ravine, Cameron came to a narrows where the only clear passage was a ten foot gap between two very large boulders.

This was the strategic point for him.

Now he heard the distant clattering of hoofs that moved towards him with the steady lope which Western horses understand, that effortless, pausing swing of the body, slower than any other gallop.

He had very little time for his preparations, but his plan was simple enough. He knotted one end of his clumsy rope around a ragged projection on the side of one boulder, then he crouched beside the other great rock with the loose end in his grip. The slack of the twisted rope lay flat on the ground.

He saw them coming. He was crouched so low that he could see the heads and shoulders of the two in the lead against the stars, so that they seemed to be sweeping through the sky. Well behind them came the third. He prayed that the last rider might be big Will Tierney!

He gauged his moment with the most precise care, then jerked up the rope and laid his weight against it. Well below the knees of the horse the rope struck. There was a jerk that hurled Cameron forward, but as he rolled he saw horse and rider topple.

The mustang was beginning to rise, snorting, and the rider lay prone and still at a little distance. Cameron caught the reins of the mustang and led it to the fallen rider. He had to lean close to make out the features of the man in the dull starlight; and with a groan he recognized Joe Peyton.

He thrust his hand inside Peyton's shirt and pressed it above the heart until he felt the reassuring pulsation. Not dead. Knocked out.

He got Peyton's gun and flung himself on the back of the horse. He was at full gallop in a moment, speeding after the distant beat of hoofs.

He rushed the horse, pressing its flanks with his spurs, and the leading pair of riders came back to him through the night, growing visible, larger and larger.

"You all right, Joe?" shouted Harry Peyton.

Cameron uttered a wordless grunt for answer, and the leaders rode on, unsuspicious.

He could distinguish them one from the other, now. Will Tierney was in the lead, Harry Peyton two or three lengths behind Tierney. Therefore it was beside him that Cameron rushed his mustang, bringing the horse up so fast that Peyton had only time to twist in the saddle and cry out once in astonishment.

A clip across the head struck with the long barrel of Cameron's revolver dropped Peyton out of his saddle.

Men said that Will Tierney feared nothing human. He must have thought, then, that half-naked Cameron was a devil and not a man; for he dropped himself low over his saddle bow, gave his horse the spur, and raced it towards the distant lights of Gallop.

Cameron had a strange feeling that luck was with him; that having helped him past the first two stages of his night's work, it would not fail him in the last, important moment.

But he found that Will Tierney was drawing away from him. The far finer horse had opened up a gap, but the greater weight of Tierney made up the difference after the first burst of speed. His mount began to flag, while the tough mustang that labored between the knees of Cameron gained steadily.

Tierney dodged through a nest of boulders. The mustang followed like a true cutting horse on the tail of a calf. Cameron was not a length behind when Tierney turned and fired straight at him.

And the mustang went down; the earth rose. Cameron's head struck fire and he fell into a thick darkness and lay still.

When he roused, at last, he was dripping with water, sloshed over him by the figure that stood tall and black against the stars. A groan passed involuntarily through the lips of Cameron.

"Coming to, kid?" asked Tierney's voice, cheerfully. "Feeling better?"

Cameron tried to move, but found that his legs and hands had been bound together with something harder and colder than twine. Then he realized that he had been bound with wire—hard bound, so that the iron ground the flesh against the bones of wrist and ankle.

He stared up at the stars and found them whirling into fire. Nearby, there was the sound of swiftly whispering water. And gradually he realized what had happened, and the sort of a death that he was likely to face.

"So I'm to go the way that Mark Wayland went, eh?" asked Cameron. "Why did you kill him? He never did harm to any man."

"He did to *me*," declared Tierney. "Five

years ago, when I was feeling pretty good, I got into a fight with a breed. I never had any use for breeds."

"I know," agreed Cameron.

He was trying to think. Mark Wayland had always said that a good brain could cut a man's way through any difficulty. What device could he find to free himself from the danger of death now? At least, he might keep Tierney talking for a little time. Every moment saved was a chance gained, in that sense.

"This breed," said Tierney, "got me down on the floor of the barroom, and I pulled out a gun and let him have some daylight through his belly. He kicked himself around in circles and took a long time to die. You never heard anything like his screaming. I hung around and listened to the last of it, and that was where I was a fool. There were half a dozen people that saw it all but they felt the way I did—that killing a breed was always self-defense. Then another man stepped in—Mark Wayland. He started for me. I pulled my gun on him, but he was a little faster."

Tierney rubbed his right arm. "Clipped me through the arm so that my gun dropped and then he turned me over to the sheriff. The sheriff didn't want to arrest me but after Wayland had done the pinching, the law started

working. Nothing but murder. And me head-
ed straight for the rope. But I managed to
work my way out of the jail, one night. That's
one of the good things about this country—
cheesecloth jails." He grinned.

"Well, after five years I got word of where
Wayland had his mine. So I went up there to
see him. I lay up behind the rocks and
watched you start out hunting. After you left,
I slipped down to the shack and slugged him
over the head. It was easy. Then I wired him,
and touched a match to his clothes to wake
him up. He wakened with a holler, too, like
the sort of a noise that lousy breed made on
the barroom floor."

It was indeed a horrible thing to look
straight into the soul of a man without the
slightest sense of right and wrong.

Big Will Tierney sat down on a convenient
rock and lighted a cigarette. "I thought he'd
break down," he said, "when I pointed out
what I was going to do—light the cabin and
let him roast like pork. But he locked up his
jaws and didn't say anything. Made me nervous, sittin' there and looking into the cold of
his eyes. It almost made me think of hell—
you know."

"And you went ahead!" muttered Cameron.

"Wouldn't I have been a fool not to? I'd found the gold in the sacks. I needed that money, and I needed it damn bad. Old Peyton was dead set against me marrying his girl unless I showed I was able to take care of her. He said he'd never put up the money for me to live easy. He's always seen through me a little. He's the only one of the Peyton family who has—until *you* came along, damn you!"

There was no particular venom in Tierney's last speech. He shrugged his shoulders and went on: "Not that I give a damn about having Jacqueline wise to me. I never cared a rap about her. But I wanted her slice of the Peyton money when it came due. That old swine has a couple of millions. Did you know that?"

"I knew he had money. Where did you kill the breed?"

"Why, it was a little side trip I made down to Phoenix. If you live till tomorrow, you're welcome to use the news wherever you please."

Tierney laughed. He had a fine, mellow-sounding laugh, and the strength of it forced back his head.

"But damn the Peyton money," he went on. "I'll get along without it. I would have had to play a part with Jacqueline all my life. Un-

51

less I decided to raise so much hell with her that the old man would buy me off with a good lump sum. But I've never had to work my way, and I never will have to. Always too many suckers around like Wayland. They dig out the coin and the wise birds like me get it." He laughed again.

"But what am I going to do about you, old son? I've got matches. How about lighting you up and watching you roast? As long as you liked Wayland so much, you might as well go to hell the way he went." He leaned over Cameron. "I think I'll have to take that pair of spurs, though," he decided. "Where'd you get golden spurs?"

"My friend gave them to me. Les Harmody."

"Well, they'll look a lot better on me."

He stepped forward to catch Cameron by one foot. His head was low. And Cameron let drive with his heels at the head of Tierney. With the golden spurs of Les Harmody he struck out, making his supple body into a great snapping whiplash.

Tierney, seeing the shadow of danger at the last instant, yelled out and tried to dodge. But the spurs tore across the flesh of his chin and the heels themselves thudded against the bone of his jaw. He fell on his face.

Cameron got the revolver from the holster at the side of Tierney first. The big fellow was already beginning to move a little as Cameron held the weapon in both hands and with two bullets severed the wires that bound his knees and ankles.

It was a harder, an almost impossible task, to get a bullet through the wires that confined his wrists. To manage that, he had to hold the Colt between his feet, pressing his wrists over the uptilted muzzle of the gun until one strand of the wire was against the muzzle. But he could not keep the flesh of the wrists from pressing over the muzzle together with the wires.

He managed to get the middle finger of his left hand over the trigger of the gun; another extra pressure and the explosion followed. Hot irons seemed to tear the soft flesh inside his wrists—but his hands were free.

And there was Tierney on his feet at last, staggering a little, then snatching at a second gun as he realized what had happened. Cameron shot low, aiming between the hip and the knee, and saw the big fellow pitch to the side. He struck on both hands, the gun spinning away. Then he reclined there as though he had been struck down by a spear and pinned to the ground.

"Cameron, don't shoot—for God's sake, don't shoot!"

Cameron went to the fallen gun and kicked it back to Tierney.

"I ought to kill you the way you were going to murder me, Tierney," he said. "But I'm not going to do that. Wayland taught me a different way. There's the gun inside your reach. Grab it. Fill your hand and take your chance."

"What chance?" groaned Tierney. "I'm bleeding to death! It'll be murder. It'll damn your soul to hell. For the sake of God, don't kill me!"

And Tierney, spilling suddenly forward along the ground, buried his face in his arms and began to groan for mercy.

That was why Cameron, sick with disgust, brought Will Tierney into the town of Gallop with the feet of his prisoner tied under the belly of the horse. A crowd formed instantly, men ran from the saloons; and someone was sent off to rouse the doctor.

Tierney, when he saw familiar faces, began to make a frantic appeal: "Bob—Sam—Bill— hey, *Bill!*—help me out of this. The damned breed shot me from behind. I'm bleeding to death! Bill, are you going to let me go like this?"

He held out his hands in appeal. Cameron rode beside him with no gun displayed. He made a picture that filled the eyes of men, however, and kept them at a distance. For blood had run and dried from a thousand scratches, and naked as he was to the waist, he looked like a savage come back from war with a captive.

Harry Peyton and the gray-headed sheriff appeared at the same time, Harry shouting: "There he is, sheriff! There he is now. I'll help you get him!"

Harry Peyton had a thick bandage around his head, and was pulling out a gun as he ran. The sheriff stopped him.

"If there's gunwork, I'll handle it."

The crowd had become thicker. Men held back from actually stopping the progress of Cameron, but they drew nearer and nearer. "Are you the sheriff?" Cameron called out.

"I am," said the other, wading through the crowd.

"Then I'm turning Tierney over to you," said Cameron. "I'm charging him with the murder of Mark Wayland."

"What's this charge of murder?" demanded the sheriff. "Are you wounded, Tierney? This looks like a black night's work for you, Cameron! Harry, help me get Tierney off his horse. Cut that rope."

Now the horses were stopped, the men pressed suddenly close from every side. There was a shout from the rear of the crowd: "Hang the damned breed! Lynch him!"

Cameron leaned from the saddle and gripped the shoulder of the lawman.

"Are you going to listen to me?" And the green glare of his eyes struck a sudden awe through the sheriff.

"I'm listening," he said "What's this talk about murder?"

"Tierney killed Mark Wayland. He confessed the killing tonight."

"Confessed? And what made him do that?"

"He got overconfident—when he had me on the ground tied with wire—the way he tied Wayland before he burned him."

"You gonna listen to a liar?" demanded Will Tierney. "I swear—he shot me from behind, like a sneaking—"

"Here's the proof," said Cameron. He held out his torn wrists, with the blood still trickling from them.

The sheriff nodded. "It's true," he said, suddenly convinced.

"And if you need more," said Cameron, "then send word to Phoenix. They've wanted

Tierney for murder there for five years. They'll want him still."

He said it loudly, and the muttering of the crowd was blanketed in a sudden silence. The sheriff said: "Look at me, Will. Is this true? Have you been a damn wolf in sheepskin, all this time?"

"Wait a minute!" yelled Tierney. "You wouldn't believe a breed against a white man's word, would you?"

"Cameron," said the sheriff, "I see I've got to thank you for doing a job I should have handled myself. Tierney, you look as guilty as hell, and hell is where you'll wind up, with a hangman's rope to start you on the way."

Cameron rode at the shoulder of the doctor, with Harry Peyton and Joe Peyton in the rear. The brothers said nothing. They were not the kind to waste words, but neither, Cameron was sure, were they the sort to nourish grudges. And that was how they arrived back to the shack where big Les Harmody was lying.

The doctor made his examination, then stepped back. "The devil's own luck, and an extra heavy set of ribs have saved you, Harmody!"

An involuntary gasp of relief broke from

the lips of Cameron and, hearing that, Harmody held out a sudden hand towards him.

"Old son!" he said.

Cameron caught the big hand and gripped it hard.

"The two of us, Les!" he exclaimed.

"Fine! said Harmody. "But suppose we make it three?"

He nodded toward the girl and she, from her place beside the bed, forced her head up until she was looking with great eyes straight at Cameron. She began to smile in a way half fond and half foolish and John Cameron knew that he had reached the end of pain.

The Fear of Morgan
the Fearless

At the age of twenty-four, in 1917, Faust sold
his first professional short story to the legendary Bob Davis, editor of *All-Story Weekly*. It
was Davis who saw the mythic potential in
Faust's fiction and encouraged the young author to write westerns. The first Max Brand
novel, *The Untamed*, was published in March
of 1919. Two months later, in June of that
year, *All-Story Weekly* printed "The Fear of
Morgan the Fearless." The mythic elements
that distinguish Faust's work are all present in
this lusty, melodramatic account of Morgan
the outlaw—but here they are tinged with
irony and an admission of human fallibil-
ity.

In this offbeat story the classic gunfighter's
showdown is given a reverse twist as heroism
becomes the stuff of vaudeville tragedy. Even
at this very early stage in his western writing
career, Faust was boldly experimenting, test-
ing the limits of Old West mythology.

Max Brand's talent as a supreme popular

storyteller, a spinner of tall tales, finds active expression here in this freewheeling saga of a fabled gunman facing his hour of crisis.

Pete's was a blessing. After you've footed it all over the city through the day, interviewed bored celebrities and listened to the barking of a city editor, quiet is a blessing. Pete's was quiet.

Of course there was the roar of the Elevated where it turned down from the Bowery just outside the door, and there was the rattling and the rumble of the surface traffic as well. But for all that, Pete's was quiet. The lights were dim and yellowish. The hissing of frying meat in the little kitchen at the end of the room was a soothing sound, and the feel of the sawdust rubbing under foot was pleasant and soothing.

Helms discovered the place. Helms was fat and subdued from a long career as a copy reader, but he was always discovering things. He mentioned the place to Crossby and me and after that the three of us rarely missed our early morning half-hour at Pete's. I don't know why he chose Crossby and me. I was only a cub and hardly knew him. Crossby was a star. I suppose it was because both of us came from the West and Pete's was decidedly Western in atmosphere. A lariat sagged over the coat-hangers the length of the room on one side. On the facing wall, high out of reach, hung a richly ornamented Mexican sombrero. Near it was a pair of silver spurs in a glass case. The spurs had belonged to Morgan.

In fact Morgan was almost like an invisible personality in the room. Pete talked of him constantly. We loved to hear the big fellow tell tales of his favorite desperado, and almost every night he gave us a new chapter.

Morgan the Fearless had performed as many heroic actions as there are pages in a book. He had bullied saloons full of gunfighters. He had held up countless stage coaches. He had plundered safes, and had shot up whole towns. The day was not finished until we had heard of an exploit of Morgan's.

We were never disappointed.

At that hour there were few customers in the place. Pete used to bring us our order and then come and take the other chair at our table. He never gave until he received. He was hungry for lurid stories, and among the three of us we always managed to give him some choice stuff. Crossby had stored away a thousand stories of revolting crimes. After a while we fell back upon him altogether.

Pete would listen with both elbows spread out on the table and his big fingers running through his drooping mustache, and into his eyes would come a peculiar dreaminess.

Then, he would talk of Morgan the Fearless, stimulating his memory or his imagination from time to time with noisy sips from a tall mug of beer. His language was a singular mixture of Western and New York slang.

But an end came to both Pete and Morgan the Fearless. It was all on account of Helms who asked the foolish question. Helms had an almost feminine curiosity. He asked Pete to tell us what had finally become of Morgan. Afterward we held it against Helms, but that night I suppose Crossby and I were equally curious. After all it was a natural question, for according to Pete, the fearless Morgan had already passed through enough adventures to secure the fame of a dozen ordinary desperadoes.

"The end of Morgan?" said Pete rather vaguely, running his pale glance from one face to the other.

"He *did* have an end, didn't he?" queried Helms.

"He sure had an end," said Pete slowly.

"This is a special occasion, you know," insisted Helms. "Crossby is going out to Chicago tomorrow and I think we ought to finish the last installment before he leaves, don't you, Pete?"

The force of this appeal was manifest at

once in Pete's eyes. Crossby was his favorite, there was no doubt of that.

"All right," said Helms, spreading his elbows out on the table in a restful attitude of attention, "let's have the death of Morgan."

Pete's eye wandered to a corner of the room and stayed there a moment.

"He *did* die, right?" asked Helms.

"Aye," said Pete. "Ole Morgan's dead, right enough."

We all waited with a curious intentness, knowing that the story was about to come. I could see Pete's plump face wrinkling a little with pain, or perhaps it was from the mere effort of memory.

"It was down at Barclay's," he began. "I've told you about the place."

"Barclay's was the road inn, wasn't it?" asked Helms.

"Yep."

"That was the saloon where Morgan drank a quart of fire water one night on a bet, wasn't it?"

"Yep," said Pete, growing more cheerful as he thought back to his older tales.

"Well, what happened?" asked Crossby.

"They'd put up with Morgan for a long time," went on Pete. "Sometimes they'd get together posses and chase him through the

64

hills. All they got was a sight of him duckin' around a curve a long ways ahead or maybe some bullets kickin' up the dust just in front of them and tellin' them to keep back, sort of polite. That was the way things stood for a long time. But Bridgewater was gettin' bigger an' bigger an' finally it got to be a city and they had their own mayor an' all that. That was how it started."

He shrugged his fat shoulders and frowned over his beer again.

"Well," he went on, "one night Morgan holds up a stage comin' into Bridgewater on the Caswell Road. It was the first stage he'd stuck up for nigh onto two months. That was the funny part of it. He just did it sort of for fun because excitement was gettin' kind of low around there an' you can all buy in on the fact that Morgan sure enough loved excitement."

"We gathered that, all right," grinned Crossby.

"I thought his finish came in the saloon, not holding up a stage?" queried Helms.

Pete regarded him with equal parts of sadness and vexation.

"I'm tryin' to tell it from the start," he said, "because if there hadn't been no holdup there wouldn't have been no finish to Morgan in the saloon. You see, when he stuck up the stage all he got was a couple of pocket watches which stopped runnin' in a few days an' a handful of silver money. That was all he got an' all he did, except to shoot the ear off the near leader as the stage was coming around the bend and to throw a fright into the mayor's daughter. That was how the trouble began, that throwing a fright into the mayor's daughter."

"Ah," said Helms. "I knew there'd be a woman in it. Was she a looker, Pete?"

"She wasn't much of anything," said Pete, in his slow voice. "Her hair was light and her skin was dark and the most she had in the way of variety was a string of freckles runnin' across her nose. Nobody ever looked twice at her in all her life, I reckon, exceptin' her father—an' her father was mayor of Bridgewater."

He stopped again for his noisy recourse to the beer mug.

"Her father was built bulgin', like a wheatsack that ain't filled tight an' sags in the middle. That was what old man Craig looked like. He ought to have been good natured, he was that fat. But he wasn't. He was the kind of guy who keeps hammering the hollow of one hand with his other fist while he's talkin' to you. That was how he got elected mayor of Bridgewater. He talked them out of their votes. He talked so much nobody else got a chance to be heard. Well, as I was sayin' he was fat enough to have been good natured, but he wasn't. He had a sort of ingrowin' grudge against the world. First thing he did when he got into office was to get them to raise the price of liquor licenses. I leave it to you, what kind of a man is that?"

Pete threw out his hands palm up in a gesture of appeal. One after another we shook our heads in solemn agreement that such a mayor was not a man at all.

"Yep," he went on, "he sure had a grudge against everything in the world except his daughter, and his daughter was the one who got scared and squealed and fainted like a young fool when Morgan held up the stage as quiet and gentlemanlike as any stage was ever held up in the Rockies. So she come home and she had hysterics all the way into Bridge-water. That was ten miles, but it didn't use her up none. She still had plenty of strength left to moan and holler around her dad. An' the old man got terrible sore.

"The next day he fired the sheriff an' told him he was no good. He wasn't no good as a sheriff, but he had a winnin' way with him an' the mayor got more unpopular than ever after he done it. But there wasn't hardly no way of disputin' the mayor. He was right. The sheriff let Morgan keep cavortin' around the country and when he went out an' chased him with a posse everyone knew that the only reason Morgan didn't stop an' hold up the sheriff an' his posse was because he had a sense of humor.

"Well, the mayor, he got some of the leadin' citizens of Bridgewater together, leavin' out the saloonkeepers, and he told them that these things would have to stop, and when they asked him what, he said: Morgan. They all agreed with him and then they asked how? But the mayor was mad. He said he was goin' to send away for the best gunfighter in the United States and get him up there after Morgan. The prominent citizens they all laughed and said there wasn't no one man in the world could round up Morgan and that the gunfighter had better be measured for a coffin before he started to work.

"But the next thing folks knew they heard that the mayor had sent to Austin, down in Texas, for a sure-enough gunpuller, a fellow known all through northern New Mexico as the best livin' imitation of the devil. Buck Christy was his name." He drained more of the beer, with us sitting in rapt attention.

"I don't know how much the mayor guaranteed to Christy if he'd come up and corral Morgan, but anyway one day a little skinny runt with a pale face and a manner that said 'Excuse me!' before he opened his mouth, this here runt got off the stage at Bridgewater an' went up to the mayor's office.

"The mayor was sittin' there with his feet on top of the roll-top desk. He was all through his day's work and was trimmin' his fingernails.

" 'Are you the mayor?' asks this little guy.

"The mayor slants an eye at him an' spits liberal into the place where the spittoon outght to have been but wasn't.

" 'I am,' says he.

" 'I'm Buck Christy,' said the stranger an' held out his hand.

"The mayor, he didn't make any move. He just sat there an' popped his eyes.

" 'You're who?' says he.

" 'I'm Buck Christy,' says this guy with the pale face.

" 'You're hell,' says the mayor, sort of comin' to life. 'Christy'd eat three or four like you before breakfast sort of as an appetizer.'

"Now the mayor was a big man an' this guy was small, an' there was a couple of clerks in the outer office who heard an' saw all this. But they didn't see anything more because the little guy he turned around an' locked the door. Afterward they heard a tolerable lot of noise in the office. Pretty soon the noise stopped an' the door opens an' the little guy comes out lookin' as pale an' sad as ever. Behind him was the mayor. He was kind of red in the face an' his collar was missin', also a large part of his right sleeve.

" 'Boys,' says he, speakin' sort of cheerful, 'this here stranger is Buck Christy that I reckon all of you've heard a lot about.'

"Christy he just stood there an' looked around at them an' somehow they all forgot to grin. They all come up and said how glad they was to meet him."

Pete sighed deeply.

"That was how Buck Christy came to Bridgewater," he went on, "an' that was the beginnin' of the end of Morgan."

"Do you mean to say that little guy finished Morgan?" queried Helms. "I thought Morgan was a big guy."

"He was," said Pete.

"And Christy finished him?" asked Helms again.

Pete shrugged his shoulders and frowned.

"Go ahead, Pete," broke in Crossby, "and

70

you shut up, Helms! You're plain spoiling the best story we've heard."

Helms relaxed into silence and Pete resumed the narrative.

"Of course every one around those parts heard about it right off. All the men out of Bridgewater started bettin' on it like it was a horse race. Harry Everett—he was the guy that Morgan found in the blizzard an' carried home—Harry Everett, he rode into Bridgewater an' offered twenty to one that Morgan would make a fool of Buck Christy.

"Christy he heard what was happenin' an' he went down to Barclay's where Harry was hangin' out.

" 'How much do you want to bet ag'in' me?' says he, goin' up to Harry.

" 'Anything you got to offer,' says Harry as quick as a flash, he bein' a real sport with an awful comeback when he was called.

" 'Well,' says Christy, 'I got a thousand that ain't doin' a thing an' I don't know anything I'd rather do with it than this.'

"So they made the bet regular, an' they wrote it down an' got the mayor to come an' witness it. That was the first time the mayor ever come into Barclay's.

"Well if there was considerable excitement about this guy Christy before it didn't let down none after that twenty-thousand-dollar bet was laid. Nobody talked of nothing else. But Christy, he didn't move. Didn't take to the trail. Just sat there in Barclay's. The mayor went to Christy one day an' told him that he had to do something quick because everybody includin' himself expected him to do something besides layin' bets on himself.

" 'There ain't nothing for me to do,' says Christy in his soft sort of voice. 'Pretty soon Morgan will come to me. Why should I go out to *him*?'

" 'How do you mean Morgan will come to you?'

" 'He'll come to me because he's proud,' says Christy. 'That's what Morgan'll do, he'll come to me because he's proud.' "

"And *did* Morgan come to him?" asked Helms.

"Well, now, I'm gettin' to that," said Pete.

He stopped again to drain the last of his beer.

"Go on, go on!" urged Crossby.

"Christy spent all the time he was awake in Barclay's," he resumed. "When any one asked him why he spent so much time there he said that he was keepin' long office hours for the sake of Morgan.

" 'Do you really think Morgan'll come in

here where there's always a crowd?' they'd go on to ask Christy.

" 'Sure,' Christy would say, 'the crowd won't stop Morgan any. He'll hear after a while that I'm waitin' for him an' then he'll come in.' "

"And Morgan came in?" We said it all three together in a sort of awed whisper. The thing was beginning to grow ghostly.

"He came in," said Pete, pausing for effect. "It was pretty near twelve o'clock at night. There were about fifteen or twenty fellows in Barclay's big room that night. They sat around and played cards an' some of them now and then went up to the bar an' got a drink at the end of a hand because there was a lot of money goin' about an' the winners was treatin' pretty general. Most of them had been playin' all evenin'. They was sort of tired outside an' heated up inside, the way you get when you've been playin' cards a long time. Nothin' seems to happen except what comes in the game an' the rest of the world it just sort of fades away and doesn't matter. Maybe you fellows know how that is."

"We sure do," said Crossby, with feeling, who had lost half a week's pay at stud poker the night before.

"There was one funny thing about that

room," went on Pete in a solemn voice. "There was a big gasoline lamp that hung from the center of the wall right over the bar. It was a mighty bright light, but right under it where the body of the lamp came there was a sort of a shadow that fell on the floor.

"All the rest of the room was lighted up as bright as day, almost.

"Well, the boys was there playin' and drinkin' as I said, when all at once the door opens quick and there stands Morgan with his two guns out and coverin' the crowd. There wasn't anything said. Somebody looked around and then got right up with his hands over his head. Then one by one they all stood up and put their hands over their heads.

" 'Boys,' said Morgan, 'I hope I ain't disturbin' you an' I won't make you uncomfortable with no long call. I ain't here to rob anybody, not even you, Mr. Barclay. All I want is this guy who was betting a thousand dollars that he would make a fool of me. Which of you is Buck Christy?'

" 'I'm Christy,' says the little guy, an' with that he stepped out and stopped in the circle of shadow under the lamp.

"Now, Christy's gun was hangin' down limp at his side the full length of his arm, an' both of Morgan's guns was lookin' him right in the face.

"I got somethin' to say to you, Morgan, an' I think it's only fair to the boys here that they should hear what I've got to say.'

" 'Well?' says Morgan, wonderin' what was comin' next, but willin' to listen, he was that pleased to have the drop on his man out of both barrels. 'I just want to tell you an' the boys that you ain't no bad man, Morgan.'

"I guess that sort of stunned Morgan an' everyone else in the room.

" 'You've just been kiddin' yourself an' the rest of these here innocent people along, Morgan. Understand?'

"Morgan didn't understand. Nor nobody else. They wouldn't have understood if they had heard it read to them in the same words out of the Bible. They saw that Christy was pullin' some sort of a game, but they couldn't make out what is was.

" 'You've done some pretty nice little jobs,' went on Christy, 'I ain't denying that, but it wasn't because you was any bad man, Morgan. Why you ain't got any more heart than a whipped pup.'

"Morgan, he just stood there and made his eyes bigger so he could look at him better. He thought maybe that Christy was tryin' some sort of new humor on him. So he waited a little while longer, and when he got through waitin' it was too late!"

Pete broke off suddenly and dropped his face into his hands with a groan.

"Steady, man," said Crossby, leaning over and putting a hand on Pete's shoulder. "We know Morgan was your friend, but let's hear the rest of it."

Pete raised his face and began again, but his voice was unsteady.

"There they stood," he went on. "There was Christy with his gun hangin' at his side and there was Morgan with both sights full on Christy's face—like this!"

He stretched both his hands before him with the elbows resting on the table and his hands took shape as if they were quivering strongly about the handles of two revolvers. And his face changed, too. It grew harder, and he scowled steadily into space as if he were narrowing his eyes to take a careful bead through the sights.

"An' Christy went on talkin' in a soft voice," said Pete, his own words dropping into a singular drawling monotone which made my flesh creep.

" 'You been doin' a lot of things more than you've got the heart for, Morgan,' he says, an' he was lookin' Morgan straight in the eye all the time.

"Now, he had a mighty pale face, but as he stood there lookin', Morgan forgot the face. All he could see was them eyes burnin' at him out of the shadow under that there gasoline lamp, an' he kept lookin' an' lookin'.

" 'You get the urge to do some wild things on the spur of the moment,' says Christy, 'an' sometimes you do 'em pretty well, but you ain't got no heart to stand up to a real man face to face.'

"He went silent, for a minute, just lookin' steady at Morgan an' then the sights of Morgan's guns began to waver just a little from side to side. It wasn't much of a waver. Maybe holdin' the guns steady in one position made his hands begin to sort of get unsteady.

"Anyway, the guns begin to stir, though they never stirred enough to get the bead off of Christy.

" 'For instance,' went on Christy, 'you're goin' to fail with me tonight, Morgan, because tonight for the first time in your life you're up against a real man, understand? Yes, you *do* understand, Morgan, you're beginning to weaken now. I can see. Everybody in this room can see it. You're beginning to weaken.'

"All the room was dead quiet as if they was expecting some move from Morgan an' he couldn't make up his mind what it might be. An' still Christy's voice went on in that damned monotone like.

" 'You never dreamed that you could ever fall down on a job, did you, Morgan? But to-night you're gettin' weak. You ain't sure of yourself.

" 'You don't find it very nice to stand here an' look a man in the eye. Why, it's like I said, you ain't got no more heart than a whipped pup, Morgan—not the heart of a squirmin' scared pup, not you!'

"An' somehow Morgan got to sayin' those words over an' over to himself. He kept sayin' 'em over an' over in his mind: 'You ain't got no more heart than a whipped pup!'

"An' then those two guns of Morgan's they begin to drop little by little. They dropped to Christy's breast and they stayed a long time over his heart, an' then they dropped until they was pointin' at Christy's feet.

"So there they was, them two, Morgan big an' Christy little, with Christy's eyes holdin' on to Morgan's an' Morgan's eyes waverin' but stickin' to Christy's eyes that was burnin' into him out of the shadow.

"And as they stood there someone in the corner began to whisper sort of hoarse like he was sayin' his prayers: 'My God!' an' then over again 'My God! My God!' If you ever heard the sound of water drippin' regular into a well that's the way those words came into Morgan's ear.

"An' then something begin to come up in his throat an' choke him an' he felt his eyes gettin' dizzy and dim.

"Then Christy he laid his own gun over on the bar, slow, without ever movin' his eyes from Morgan's and then he made one slow step and then he took Morgan's guns out of his hands one after the other very slow an' careful, an' Morgan just stood there an' didn't make a move, with his hands still out in front of him as if he was still holdin' the guns in them.

"Then, Morgan, he sort of woke up with a start an' the room got bright to him all at once. He saw what had happened an' saw his own guns in Christy's hands. He made a sort of jump for them, but Christy, he didn't shoot, he just made a step back an' swung one gun so that the muzzle of it hit Morgan over the left eye. It didn't knock him down, but it cut him bad an' it was enough to stop him and send him back another pace. An' that's how it ended."

"But what became of him?" Helms insisted. "Did they arrest him then? Did he serve a term? And how did he die?"

"They tried to arrest him," said Pete, "But Christy wouldn't let them. He held them off, an' Morgan went outside an' got on his horse an' rode away."

"Rode *where?*" asked Helms.

"To hell!" said Pete, and he stood up. "It's closin' time."

We got up and went silently and hastily out of the room. The doors closed behind us as if they were shutting on a death.

We never saw Pete again. Never went back to his place after that night. And eventually he closed down. We heard he'd moved back West somewhere.

But one thing I'll always remember—something I hadn't noticed until that last night. Pete had gone deadly pale after he'd finished Morgan's story—and his pallor revealed, clear as anything, a scar on his forehead.

Over his left eye.

Dark Rosaleen

Again we encounter, in this fine novelette, another of Frederick Faust's gallant, wind-swift wonder horses, a steed fit for the gods, able to drift over mountain and prairie like a running dream, inspiring frustration, awe, and desire.

Faust's love for fine horses endured throughout his life (he would often ride in Central Park when he was in New York), and his great gift as a writer enabled him to transfer this love to a printed page. The special care he took in fashioning the tale of Dark Rosaleen is reflected in the fact that it was serialized in the top-quality pages of *Country Gentleman*. The story's emotional content is genuine and deep-rooted. Faust was writing from his heart—and this stalwart western finds him at the peak of his form.

Her mother's name was June, and she had been christened Sally by the slim hand of the colonel's daughter. But who could refer to Sally, the daughter of June, without running the two names together? So it was that the good mare came to be known as Sally June. To Col. Tom Savary, as he sat upon the stool in the corner of her box stall, she was perfection in horseflesh, for she had the virtues of mustang and thoroughbred; the leathery endurance of the one without its withered neck and lumpy head, the gallant heart and some of the speed of the other without its hair-trigger temper. But more than the beauty of her body, to the colonel, was her eye, for it was like the eye of a woman who is loved and loves again.

She was irascible and nervous on this day. Sometimes she wandered into the small corral which opened off her stall; and with the silken chestnut of her back mottled by the shadow of the twisted old oak tree she remained a moment looking over the burned, brown stretches of the ranch to where the mountains arose in all the north and west, clothed by distance in blues so delicate that sometimes they seemed no more than clouds and sometimes they quite melted into the sky. Then, as though annoyed that she might not be bathing in the illusive coolness of those peaks, she pawed with a dainty forefoot until the alkali of the dust she raised stung her nostrils. After that she would come back to the roomy stall, cock one ear at the sweet hay in her manger, taste it, refuse it, and finally come to a pause before her master to beg for sugar and to examine him half petulantly, half lovingly. At such times he did not pat her soft nose, for he was a man of few caresses, even for his daughter Nell, but he always had a word for Sally June, spoken in a voice with such overtones of gentleness that both her ears pricked to listen. Yet, when she moved away again, his glance would fall to her knees and his face darken.

For, alas, there was the flaw in that perfect creature, and how terrible a flaw it was. She was completely broken down in both front legs, so that even when she tried to hurry with the others in the pasture her gallop was a hobbling, painful thing to see. Yet once she had frolicked away from the fleetest of them all, looking back in scorn as they followed her with their ears flattened by their speed. Such was Sally June as Nature intended her; such she was when the colonel told himself that the Comanche Cup was as good as in his hands and his great ambition satisfied. But, a month before the race in which she was entered, a drunken stable boy had taken her out without orders, run her a wild journey across the lava flow which lay to the east of the ranch and brought her back a hobbling wreck. The colonel had given her one look on that black day and then gone into his room to sit till the next morning with his head in his hands and murder in his heart.

So vanished his hopes for the Comanche Cup for that year, and the blow was the greater since Sally June was the product of careful breeding, not of happy chance. The colonel had conceived the idea of the race, for he saw that what the West needed was a horse which was more agile and enduring than the thoroughbred, but faster than the cow pony, and larger; and no races over flat country or a smoothed track would call such an ideal into existence. So he picked out Comanche Pass from During to Las Gatas, twenty miles of steep slopes, rocks, and a trail more wildly looped than a tangled lariat, concluding with five more miles of soft, thick sand. Sure footing, cool nerves and a wise head for the broken trail in the mountains; indefatigable patience for the stretch of sand; and combined with these a great heart for pressing always on at the best possible speed—these were the requirements in horseflesh for the running of

Comanche Pass.

The big ranchers took up the idea at once with enthusiasm. There were plenty of silver cups as prizes, so they put up a sixty-pound gold cup as the permanent trophy to go to the first man who won the race three times. The colonel, as though fortune wished to favor the originator of the scheme, won the first two races. But after that he had worse luck. For the ranchers spared no pains to write their names at least once upon the side of that cup. They discovered a formula which produced the ideal horse for the heartbreaking work in the Pass; they crossed the finest strains of thoroughbred blood upon the rawest mustang stock they could find. The result was a generation of horses tough as steel and fleet as the wind; but the colonel, surpassing their efforts, imported an Arab mare at huge expense, and Sally June was her daughter, not by a racing stallion, but by a wise-headed old hunter who had carried a 200-pound rider for eight years without a serious fall!

It was small wonder, then, that when Sally June broke down the colonel passed into a black despair; but he was a man who took much beating. He bred Sally June to the same hunting strain; and the reason that she was fretful this day was that the moment of birth must come within the next two days; and the reason that the colonel was absent-minded was that he was lost in a bright dream of the Comanche Cup as it would appear in his library with the picture of the winner above it.

One of his grooms appeared at the door.

He was an imported servant, for the colonel had discovered long since that a cowpuncher is too apt to treat his mount as a means of conveyance simply and not as a friend and companion, and therefore he had brought in a working corps of English grooms to take charge of his breeding operations. It was one more of those steps in pursuit of the Comanche Cup that had wiped out his banked surplus and left a deficit which he had had to cover with mortgages.

"Word comes up from town, sir, that Sam Toomey is about, drinking, and swearing he'll be even with you."

"Quite so," said the colonel. "Thank you, Motherell."

He had not heard a word; he was saying to himself that the picture of Sally June must appear together with the picture of her colt above that gold cup. But Motherell, who knew the mind of his master by the dream in his eyes, repeated the message:

"Word has come that Toomey is in town

threatening you and drinking hard, sir."

"Very good, Motherell," said the colonel; but he was telling himself that when the Comanche Cup was his, his wife would worry no longer about those piling debts, the thought of which had worn her thin. It would mean four years of waiting, but what are four years to a man who loves horses?

"Toomey is in town threatening to get even with you, sir, and getting very drunk," said Motherell for the third time.

The colonel started like a man awakened from deep sleep. "Toomey?" he said. "Toomey? Get even with me? The low rascal, if he were to lay down his life he couldn't make up for the harm he's done me!"

For Toomey had ridden Sally June and broken her on that sad day long ago.

The colonel had risen from his stool and struck his hands together.

"The whipping post! The whipping post!" He exclaimed. "The whipping post, Motherell!"

Motherell blinked at him with rounded eyes, but when the Colonel was moved he was rarely clear in his speech.

"That's what Toomey needs. By gad, I'd like to be the executioner. I'd relish it. I'd relish laying the lash on his back till he bled."

"Shall we have Toomey watched?" asked Motherell.

But the colonel brushed past him and went into the dusk which was gathering thick over the ranch to walk up and down until the passion left him, and he answered Motherell not a word.

After dinner he came out to say good night to Sally June, to look to her bedding, to see that the water in her little private trough was fresh, and that the zinc lining of the trough itself was new-scoured so that it shone under the lantern light. He had gone back into the house before Nell Savary started on the same errand. She did no examining, however; she merely sat on the edge of the manger and took the head of Sally June in her arms and whispered in her ear. For the colonel's wife was a bedridden invalid and the colonel himself was kinder of voice than of hand, and Nell and Sally June had to make up to each other for the petting which they got from no one else. Ever since Sally June came into the world she and Nell had not missed a good-night talk, and after the talk, as always, Nell went back to the house and whistled softly and the mare whinnied her answer. Then the screen door slammed with a faint rattle; the house door closed quietly. The night had begun.

Then it was that Sam Toomey came forth from the shed in which he had waited and watched. Whisky had not addled the brain behind his cramped forehead; it had merely given a single clear purpose to his malice, and he went straight to the stall of Sally June.

She snorted and shook her head at him, for she remembered him well, but when he held out the halter, she pushed her head obediently into it. She had learned that first of all lessons for horseflesh, that the voice of the man must be obeyed simply because it is man who speaks. When the rope tugged at the halter she turned and followed at once; for that other lesson which all ranch horses must know had been conned by rote by Sally—she must not pull back against a rope.

She followed to the gate of the corral, then through it and on to the little shed at the verge of the ranch buildings. There, in the darkness, another horse waited, saddled and bridled, which Toomey mounted and jogged off into the night with Sally June following with her painful hobble.

The wind rose behind them, freshening each moment. It was a half gale when Toomey paused at the crest of the first hill and looked back to the hollow and the clear yellow shining of the windows of the rancher's house.

How huge its black outlines were! And at the thought of the money it had cost and the power it represented, Toomey snarled like a beast and spurred his horse down the farther slope. Sally June followed as best she might.

Before that wind blew over, in the gray of the next morning, it had whipped the desert with a sandstorm that made man and beast scurry for shelter and crouch where they found it, cupping their hands over mouth and nose that they might breathe without being choked by the flying dust. But desert dust will almost drift through a solid wall; certainly it had no trouble silting through the cracks between the boards of the long freight train which was rattling eastward that night and morning, carrying Mark Lupin toward safety.

There were sixty "empties" in that caravan, and every boxcar was filled with an atmosphere of dull red mist, a choking, blinding mist of dust. Lupin had endured it half the night simply because he dared not risk the open force of the wind, but when the light began, though the wind was still heavy, he pushed the sliding door of the car back and clambered up to the roof. The gale died; the sun rose; and sprawled on the top of the car the brakeman found Lupin.

He was not a kindly man, this "shack," and being by nature vicious, he was more savage than usual this morning, since he had been harried all the night by the inescapable flying silt. What he intended when he first saw Lupin was to take him by one foot and pitch him from the top of the car. If the fall crushed his shoulder or broke his back the vision of his writhings would never haunt that brakie: in fact, he had done the same thing more than once before. But as he drew nearer Lupin coiled himself into a sitting posture, resting his weight on his toes and looking full in the other's face, without fear. He was full inches shorter than the trainman, being not more than middle height, and he lacked much of the latter's bulk; but there was something in his wide shoulder, his long arms, and above all in the catlike smoothness of his movements, that made the brakeman alter his first intention. The nearer he came to the pale blue eyes of Lupin the more certain he became that this fellow was, at the least, a tramp royal and not to be tampered with carelessly. So he grinned down into the face of Lupin where the red desert dust clung in a stubble of beard and gave him good morning.

"What are you doing up here?" asked the shack.

"Here's what," answered Mark Lupin, and he dipped a broad silver dollar out of his coat pocket and gave it to the other. The brakie juggled it a moment in his horny palm.

"That's reason enough," he said, and slid the coin into his trousers pocket. "A rotten night, eh?"

Lupin shrugged his shoulders; his eyes were still busy reading the face of his companion with a peculiar energy. What he saw there seemed to reassure him.

"Yep, rotten," he answered tersely.

"The birds that had to live out that wind in the desert," said the shack, "must of got theirs."

At this Lupin gazed across the sands to the ragged edge of the horizon where the mountains rose; among them must be many a place where a man could lie in safe hiding.

"I don't know that it's so bad," he said wistfully, and taking off his hat he passed his hand thoughtfully over his head. The prickling of that short-cropped hair startled him back to awareness, and he clapped the hat back into place; but the shack had seen and noted.

"Just out, eh?" he chuckled. "I thought it was something like that. I done a fiver myself. At Sing Sing. Where were you?"

"Quentin," said Lupin tightly.

"I *knew* it!" replied the brakie. "Silver dollars ain't so frequent outside of California. What did they run you up for?"

Lupin gazed gloomily across the desert, not answering. Far ahead of the train a down-headed horse was stumbling slowly along near the tracks.

"Speaking of San Quentin," said the brakie, seeing that the tongue of his new acquaintance was not so loose as his own, "I see where one of the boys busted out a few days back?"

"That so?" yawned Lupin, but his pale blue eyes flickered sidewise at the shack.

"Slugged a guard and skidded for the hills. They ain't caught him yet."

"Maybe they never will."

"Oh, they will, right enough. They always do."

Now the train was closer to the crippled horse. The brakeman shook his head.

"That old nag went through the gaff last night!" he said, pointing before him.

The engine was laboring at a snail's pace up a steep grade and Lupin, turning, regarded the horse. The poor creature went on at a stumbling, hobbling pace with its head far sunken.

"Mare in foal!" cried the shack with sudden excitement. "Hanged if it ain't—and all in—

just about all in! Crazy for water—no water near—colt about to be born—why, pal, they'll both kick out! There ain't a chance for either of 'em!"

He was staring with pity and anxiety, but Lupin smiled.

"When men are treated the way they are, what d'you expect for horses?

The brakeman drew a step back as though to get a better view of his man and instinctively he hooked his hand over the lapel of his coat. Inside the coat his revolver was hung, almost as easy of access to a praticed man as if it swayed in an open bolster at his hip.

"Look at the poor old girl," he said, "just about out, but still plugging along. Hanged if she ain't broke down in front too! That's why she hobbles that way. But she ain't quitting. You notice that? She's working just as if she knew that she had to get to help—not for her own sake, but for the colt's!"

The train was roaring past the mare now, gathering speed as the engine topped the grade and lurched along the down slope beyond, and the horse had stopped and turned inward as she saw the two men on top of the car. Her fallen head she raised high, as though hope had given her strength for an instant; her flagging ears pricked, and now she neighed high and sharp above the loud rushing of the train.

The neigh of Sally June had broken in the middle and quavered away to nothing as though all of her strength had been put into that final effort. Her head fell at the same time, and now she stood swaying, her legs braced.

"D'you see it?" cried the brakeman to Lupin.

"Go on, jump down there and give her a hand."

"The devil I will! She'll feed the buzzards—her *and* her colt."

"Well, mebbe I can help change yer mind!" snarled the brakeman, jerking out his revolver. He struck down with the long, heavy barrel of the gun. It landed fairly along the head of Lupin, dropped him upon his face on the slanting roof of the car, and from this he rolled over and fell loosely upon the cinders beneath.

Mark Lupin lay sprawled beside the track for a long time, and when consciousness finally came back to him his brain was spinning, so that when he opened his eyes he shut them again hastily to close out the sparks of fire that whirled just above him. Something was pulling at his hair.

At this he wakened and sat bolt upright to find that he was confronting the cocked ears and the big bright eyes of a newborn colt. Lupin swayed to his feet with an oath, and though the effort shot burning pains through his head he remained standing. His limbs were sound, and having thoroughly stretched and tried himself to make sure of this, he looked about him at the horizon. In three quarters of the compass there extended the misty line of flat desert; in the fourth quarter arose the sacred blueness of the mountains which meant safety if he could reach them, it seemed to Lupin. He set his teeth for the effort across the hot sands, noting at the same time that the sun was nearing the zenith; there was only half the heat of the day remaining to be endured. Then he turned his glance to things nearer him. At his feet lay the last of poor Sally June, as though she had struggled toward him in her agony. Here was the colt, circling eagerly around the man. With her mother dead, instinct had taken her to the first living creature.

She was nibbling hungrily at the hand of Lupin.

"Get back!" growled Mark Lupin. And he raised his hand threateningly, but the colt seemed to take that as a signal for play. She gamboled away on her shaking legs and reeled back again with her head cocked jauntily upon one side.

"Keep off me!" grunted Lupin with an oath.

And he kicked the poor creature in the side and sent it flat on the sand with a squeal of pain and dismay. Then Lupin faced toward the northern mountains, tightening his belt. He had not eaten for more than twenty-four hours. He had not slept for two days. But these, it seemed to him, were very slight disadvantages. And the pain of his parched throat was no more than a sharp sauce to set off the sweetness of life. He had lost another trick; that was all. Had he not quarreled with the brakeman over that infernal old mare he would by this time have been another hundred miles to the east. However, what is a hundred miles compared with the thousand-league strides of the telegraph? Perhaps he would have rolled into the next station yard only to be pulled off the train by the waiting detectives. At least this was his manner of consoling himself as he struck toward the distant heights.

He swung away with the long rolling stride of an expert walker, but before he had covered fifty yards there was a pattering of hoofs behind him and he turned to confront the colt once more; it winced away from him but did not flee, for its first lesson in the pain of living had not yet taken effect on the new brain. Lupin considered the facts coldly: The mother was dead, the belly of the colt was empty, there was not even water near by and accordingly it must die in torment. He was not unwilling to grant it a final mercy, so he stooped over and picked up a ragged-edged piece of slaty rock; then he stretched out his other hand and the colt ran in to him at once. Lupin raised the rock high and chose the place between the ears where he would strike, but he hesitated. It had just come to him as a wonderful thing that the new brain of the colt should have understood that gesture of amity with which he had invited it in to him. However, he tightened his grip on the rock and set his teeth.

Still he delayed, for it was impossible to look down without encountering the large, bright, wistful eyes of the colt. At length, however, he concentrated only upon the mark at which he aimed; and then it occurred to him that his first blow might not destroy all life at once. There might be a need of a second or a third. He might have to maul the little creature to death!

The rock fell from the numbed hand of Lupin. He passed it, trembling, across his forehead and wiped away the sweat which had sprung out there.

"You damn little fool!" he cried hoarsely. "I don't mean you any good!"

He leaned, cast a handful of dust into the face of the little chestnut, and then made off at a run across the desert. He covered half a mile at close to his full speed, but at the end of that distance, the sound of the small hoofs began again behind him; the colt had followed.

Lupin sat down upon a rock which thrust out of the red surface of the sand, lighted a cigarette and considered the creature before him. The daughter of Sally June was swaying a little on her long legs, and now, with her head cocked a bit to one side, she began to move around and around the man. She had received the second lesson and she was beginning to know fear.

"My God!" cried the fugitive suddenly, "you think I'm your *mother!*"

And so stunned was he by this new thought that the cigarette fell from his fingers. At length he rose, turned again to the blue and distant heights and resumed his journey. The colt grew bolder, followed more closely, and sometimes it even tapped its forehoofs against his heels, but Lupin did not turn. He merely set his jaw the harder. The last year had taught him that there was no more pity in this world than there was justice; the colt must die; and he, Lupin, was a fool because the thought of that death tormented him. Finally, however, the little chestnut must fall behind him.

The time came, indeed, when the swishing of the sand behind him began to grow fainter, still fainter, and Lupin paused, looking back.

The daughter of Sally June was still working gallantly toward him, but her head had fallen now, her knees were buckling, and it seemed to Lupin that he was watching the mare again as she had struggled up the side of the railway track. Up to Lupin came the little straggler and sank down with sides pumping like bellows.

"What'll I do?" groaned Lupin. "Heaven above, what'll I do?"

He leaned and took the head of the colt in his hands, whereat the dimming eyes of exhaustion were turned up to ask his help. He stood. The colt made a vain effort to follow his example, but it could only stir up a dust.

"Lie still!" muttered Lupin. "You little fool, lie still. I—I'll do something!"

He ran to the top of the next rise of ground

with the colt calling sadly after him, and there in the wide and shallow hollow beyond he saw a ranch house, surrounded by its sunburned attendant shacks.

Lupin ran straight on toward it. He had come to the front gate with the dusty patch of garden beyond and a sallow-faced woman gaping at him from the doorway, before he realized what his appearance must be. The blood from the place where the muzzle of the revolver had cut his scalp had flowed down one side of his face and dried there. Red dust and sand were ingrained on his clothes. His hat was crushed from his fall from the top of the boxcar. And, in addition, he had come running from the heart of the desert in this land where men were never seen on foot.

No wonder that the housewife screamed and fled at his approach.

Lupin stepped through the door. "I'll pay for what I get!" he called, but when he received no answer he went on to the kitchen and helped himself. He found a large quantity of canned milk. That would have to serve his purpose with the colt. For himself he took some packages of raisins, some bread, flour, salt and coffee. He stole a pot and a pan as well, and around his waist he buckled a belt and hung a filled canteen at his hip. Thus equipped he left the place and hurried away with his disordered pack jangling and jouncing behind his shoulders.

The chestnut had come to its feet and had made a pace or two along his trail, but at the sight of him what a wild whinnying of delight it set up and how its short tail thrashed from side to side! The heart of Lupin rose into his throat.

He opened a can of milk with his knife, poured the contents into the pan and mixed the milk with water. That was only the beginning of the work. He had to teach the youngster to drink as he had seen new calves taught, giving it a finger to suck and then dipping its muzzle into the milk. But finally that milk was disposed of, when the patience of Lupin was worn away and a sweat of anger was on his face.

Then he sat down and made a meal on his own account. Before he had finished the chestnut was hunting for more nourishment, and Lupin regarded it with despair. If it consumed milk at such a rate, how was he to keep it alive?

Before darkness the colt was transformed. She began to frolic across the sands, tossing her head and tail and racing back to Lupin at the end of every circle. Twice more that afternoon she had required feeding, but the profit of the food was shown in her dancing eyes and in her arching neck. She was as teachable as a dog. In that short interim she learned to come when her companion whistled, and learned to stand like a rock when Lupin hissed faintly between his teeth.

When the night came she lay down, more like a dog than ever, at the feet of Lupin in the sand and fell asleep; but the fugitive waked her, and when he started over the hill toward a ranch house the daughter of Sally June followed at his heels, far too sleepy for any frolic now.

It was easy to find a corral, it was easy to put the colt through the gate, but when the gate was closed again the trouble began. For the youngster fell into a frenzied panic. She dashed up and down the fence, whinnying wildly; the instant Lupin stepped to her she snuggled her nose into the man's hand and snorted her content.

"Here's your new home," said Lupin, rubbing the silken softness of the neck. "Don't you understand that? Here's where you hang out from now on. They'll take care of you— somehow. They'll teach you manners—with a whip. They'll ride you groggy after their cows. But it's the best I can do for you, partner. I have my own hide to look after."

So he hurried off into the dark, but before he had taken a dozen steps there was a crash and a whinny of pain. He ran back and found that the colt had jumped the low gate and now was hung up on the topmost board. There was power in those long arms of Lupin to tear that board away and lift the colt across to the outside like a child. He lighted a match. A nail had slashed the colt's skin open, and blood was oozing from the cut. It seemed to Lupin that the blood made the last tie between them and sealed it fast. He scooped up a handful of dust and pressed it against the wound, and the colt stood steady, only turning its head to sniff at the ministering fingers which, with such mysterious suddenness, had caused the pain to cease.

Then slowly, slowly, for fear that long steps might open the wound in which the dust had clotted the blood, Lupin started on, and the colt followed with her muzzle close to the hand of her master.

That night they bivouacked in a dry gully in a nest of rocks between which the sand was soft and deep. Lupin dropped into a stunned sleep the instant he closed his eyes.

When he wakened, the sun was high and bright, and human voices were rolling heavily toward him. He crept to an opening among the rocks and looked out to see two riders pressing up the hollow on dusty, sweating horses. The colt stumbled to its feet, but he raised his hand and hissed softly at it, and the little creature stood frozen in place as though it had heard a word and understood.

"We're playing the fool," said one rider, "going along like this when we got no sign to guide us."

"That's the sign we need to guide us," answered the other, and waved before him.

"You mean the mountains? You mean he'll make for them?"

"Of course he will. Where else can he go? And there'll be others besides us combing the foothills for him. He'll never get through to the upper peaks."

They drifted on, their spurs jingling, their stirrup leather groaning, and Lupin felt that the trap had already closed upon him. How many years for breaking prison? How many years, and every year worse than a death! But, as the pair had said, which way could he head save toward the mountains?

So they trudged on through that day, and that night he raided another place for food for himself and milk for the colt. The colt was no handicap now. She could travel at the heels of

Lupin all day and frisk away to the sides and gallop ahead and swoop back around her master. In the afternoon they came upon a road, and since it was deserted for miles in each direction, Lupin ventured to take it to the first crossing. There, on the signpost, he found the notice posted which offered $500 for the apprehension of Mark Lupin and described him.

It was not a printed poster but had been scratched in big rough letters with a pen and was signed with the name of Newton Carey, sheriff. Lupin, in a passion, ripped down the notice and tore it to bits.

That evening they came beneath the foothills. In half an hour they were climbing, in half an hour more they came to the mouth of a cañon which drive straight into the heart of the hills. Here Lupin paused. The easiest way was down the floor of the valley, of course, but because it was the simplest and most probable route there was all the more danger that it would be watched: moreover, a moon which had been brightening the sky unseen, now slid above the eastern peaks and gilded the west wall of the rock with silver. If spies were there, they would be easily seen, while the slopes on either side of the valley were entangled with tall shrubs to screen them; however, those slopes were so perilously steep that it would be trying work indeed for the weak-legged foal to labor up them, and for the sake of the chestnut Lupin struck down the gorge.

For a quarter of a mile he went with his heart in his throat; but when the silence remained unbroken and the peaceful moon drifted higher and higher like a silver bit of wind-lifted cloud, he forgot his fears and began to sing softly to himself while the colt canted its head to listen to this new and pleasant voice from the master. He turned, still singing, when he heard a faint sound drumming behind him and then he saw the figure of a horseman blackly silhouetted against the western wall and galloping at full speed. He glanced to the farther side. Two more men were riding down upon him among the eastern shadows and still more rushed straight down the throat of the pass. There was no help for it. The colt had swung around to eye the pursuers, and Lupin took the small, soft head in his arms and then raced for the cañon wall.

He reached it and started up the precipitous face. Where there was no foothold his long and powerful arms helped him, and he swung up like a monkey from crevice to crevice. In the meantime the rush of hoofs drew nearer; he heard voices shouting, though the echoes blurred the spoken words, but what made Lupin pause on the dizzy verge of the cliff and look back was the pitiful whinnying of the daughter of Sally June. He saw her at the foot of the rock, trying gallantly and vainly to clamber up the smooth front of the cliff.

Then a wicked humming whirred close to his ear followed by the loud and metallic clanging of a rifle. And Lupin turned again to his work. He had not an instant's peace after that. Just below the cliff the hunters had gathered and with their rifles at rest they were sharpshooting at him. No doubt he would have been picked off instantly had he not been on the shadowy side of the gorge, so that the very brightness of that moon helped to secrete him. At last he gained the topmost ledge and, lying on his belly, peered over the side to the scene beneath him.

The rifles crackled no longer, though the last echoes they had roused were still speaking dimly from cliff to cliff. But the riders were now working at an easier business.

From the shadow, where it fell steepest and thickest, the colt darted into the moonshine with a horseman at its heels; the thin shadow of the rope leaped out, the noose opened, hung an instant and fell as swift as lead, but it only tapped the shoulder of the little chestnut. She had veered to the side, nimble-footed as a gazelle. That rope must be coiled before it could be flung again; but alas, there were many enemies crowding about her now! She had dodged from one danger straight into the face of another, for a second rider hurled his lasso like a bullet, almost as fast and as straight. The colt stopped on braced legs, jumped stiffly to the side and then on again out of this trap, brushing past the very side of the rider and racing away with ears flattened.

Lupin sprang up in admiration and waved his hands, shouting incoherent encouragement. Yet he knew that the fight was lost before it well began. They were scurrying around the youngster like hawks stooping at a frightened sparrow and now they cast no longer for the neck but for the feet. Even as Lupin cheered a coil fell on the ground before the foal, and she went down head over heels.

"They've killed her!" whispered Mark Lupin to himself. "Damn them!"

But the chestnut was not dead. She was only stunned by the fall and presently she clambered to her feet, kicked the coil away and darted forth once more. Now, however, they were only toying with their captive. She had hardly started before the rope fell around her neck, and when she came to the end of the lariat she was flung down again. She got up fighting like a little tigress, but that resistless band was clamped around her throat shutting off the life-giving air. And presently Lupin saw the group of horsemen depart with the colt dragged at the end of a rope, pulling back till she was choked into submission or jerked forward upon her knees.

And when the group vanished in the moon haze down the gorge, Lupin sank down upon the rock, weak with horror and grief.

Sheriff Newton Carey was a little old man who was in reality even smaller and older than he looked; which is to say that he was actually nearer seventy than sixty and that the width of his shoulders and the straightness of his back disguised his withered body. He was a man so nervous that he appeared calm, but the illusion of calm was caused merely by the immense effort he expended all his life to keep his nerves under check.

No one knew the sheriff. There were times when he felt that he did not understand himself, but that the guiding power in his life consisted of a violent spirit which resided in him but which was not a part of him. For instance, in all ordinary times he detested gambling and gamblers, but the moment his wallet began to appear fat with bills, then the demon within him hounded him to a gaming table and there he was sure to depart with cleaned hands. He had been sheriff for nearly forty years. And some people thought that he would keep on being sheriff to the end of time.

On this day he sat upon the topmost rail of a corral fence and, though every nerve in his body was jumping, he forced his hand to remain steady as he whittled at a stick of soft pine.

His brother stood at the fence behind him. Jonathan was just the reverse of Newton Carey in every way. He was much less famous, for instance, but he was far richer, a solid citizen.

"Brother," he was saying on this afternoon, "might it be that you're sick?"

The sheriff shook his head.

"Because," continued Jonathan, like one to whom an answer is not necessary, "folks are talkin' a bit; quite a bit! They're saying that it looks a doggone lot like you was just setting here these three days watchin' the colt."

And he waved his hand to a little chestnut foal which was walking up and down the corral fence and sometimes stopping to stretch its head between the bars and whinny sharp and shrill.

"Of course," pursued Jonathan, "me and them that knows you thinks different."

"I'm glad you know me, brother," said the sheriff in a smooth voice.

"We think different," said Jonathan, "because I know that no brother of mine would be such a fool. Not while there's an outlaw wanderin' around through the mountains. But still there's them that talks and talks!

"To put it short, brother, them that are talking says that there must be some reason why you called off all them that was hunting this Lupin gent. They guess maybe that you know why he shouldn't be caught."

The sheriff spoke at last.

"Look yonder to the colt," he said.

"I see, I see," snapped Jonathan.

"What might you think?"

"About the colt? I dunno that she ain't too thin in the legs and too long in the legs to make much of a cow hoss. Kind of pretty made, though. Where'd Lupin pick that colt up?"

The sheriff countered with a question.

"Where would that there snip of a hoss go if it was turned loose?"

"How can I tell?" asked Jonathan.

"Well, it looks like she was trying to get somewheres."

"Trying to get back to Lupin, maybe."

"Maybe Lupin," said the sheriff dreamily, "is trying to get back to her. Eh?"

"Lupin trying to get back to her? I ask you, is that sense, Newton?"

"I ask you," rejoined the sheriff, "is it sense for hossflesh to be takin' on for a man like that man was her mother?"

Of this Jonathan could make nothing.

"I dunno that I can say more," he said finally. "I've come and give you warning, Newt. That's all I can do. I've told you the talk that's going around. It's things like this that make a gent lose office. And if you wasn't sheriff, what would you be, Newt?"

The sheriff made no reply, but he raised his head and squinted at the pale horizon. When he looked down again, Jonathan was hastily striding away.

"I need that five hundred reward all for myself, Jonathan," he said to the departing figure. "And I need it bad. That's why I'm sitting here watchin' a colt!"

For a man's gambling debts are the debts which live ever nearest his heart, and the sheriff owed a certain Mexican nearly four hundred as a result of an all-night session at poker.

He left the corral for supper. After supper he went back to his post, but this time he chose a shelter under a bush some ten yards from the fence, and there he waited with his back to the trunk and his legs doubled under him. He watched for two hours. In the meantime the colt had dropped down to sleep for a time, but presently it was up again, pacing up and down the fence, up and down as a wolf paces for a year after captivity. At last it stopped.

It had seen or heard something, and what it had heard now came to the ear of the sheriff, a hiss like the hiss of a snake, infinitely soft. Then a shadow glided around the corner of a shed, slipped up to the corral, and Newton Carey saw the foal rear up like a dog and plant her forehoofs on the top rail.

"Lupin!" he called, and snatched for his gun.

The shadow at the corral fence dropped to the ground, wavered toward the shed from which it had come, then changed its course and swerved toward the sheriff, and Newton Carey fired. The shadow dodged; he fired again and still it came veering in to him, elusive as a snake's tail that whips through grass, and fully as fast. It closed on him. One hand of iron seized his right wrist and the wrist turned to fire, the gun dropped from the fingers. Another hand caught him by the throat, and he went down.

The man above gasped out an oath, "It's an old man!"

He stood up from the sheriff, took a pace or two, and then sank into the dust.

When the men came from the bunk house and from the ranch with lanterns and shouts and gleaming guns, they found the sheriff working to apply a tourniquet to the leg of Lupin, for Lupin it was who lay in the dirt bleeding from a bullet wound.

On the day of Mark Lupin's capture, she had broken free of the corral and disappeared into the hills. Running wild, as a yearling she was a shining beauty, a black chestnut, more black than red, with a dapple like the marking of a jaguar over her sleek body. As for her mane and tail, they were black silk, and when Jerry Flynn saw her flying across the field the lines of a song rang in his brain:

The Erene, at its highest flood,
   I dashed across unseen,
  For there was lightning in my blood,
   My Dark Rosaleen,

My own Rosaleen!
Oh, there was lightning in my blood
My Dark Rosaleen!

And in that instant, Jerry Flynn christened her Dark Rosaleen.

She was a lonely creature, and when the other horses in the herd merely tossed their heads as a cowpuncher ranged in view, Dark Rosaleen never failed to take to her heels and gallop until the intruder had dropped below the horizon; for she had not forgotten that moonlit gorge where she had first seen riders wielding in their hands inescapable ropes that burnt like coils of flame.

At first the loneliness of the desert hills would drive her back to the rest of the herd, but by degrees she discovered that the desert itself has presences and voices. Indeed, practically all of her desert wisdom, which was to grow at last into a rich, thick book, she gained by herself on lonely wanderings.

From the day when she tried to catch the far horizon and discovered that that amazing pale circle could run away as fast as she could gallop toward it to the day when she conducted her investigation of a pair of grizzly cubs, Dark Rosaleen learned everything with her own sharp wits alone as tutor. Twice she came within an ace of losing her life.

The affair of the two cubs was the first narrow escape. She had come upon them in a narrow arm of the ravine, and her first glimpse was of two balls of fur darting into one end of a hollow log.

Presently a tiny, shiny black nose appeared at the end of the log, shrank away, appeared again, and then a cub stepped boldly forth followed at once by its brother. They reared upon their haunches after the fashion of bears and regarded her gravely, almost weeping with fear and curiosity.

Presently they rolled off their haunches and began to move in a circle to investigate Rosaleen. Finally they sat down together like two errant little boys and looked up into her face.

Dark Rosaleen stealthily lifted a forehoof. She had learned to strike with that hoof as quickly as a cat dabs with its paw. And she intended to test the hardness of the head of the cub upon the right. But, just as the impending danger was hanging in the air and about to fall, something for which Dark Rosaleen could never account made her plant that hoof again and leap violently to one side. And as she leaped, the mother grizzly rushed past from behind with a roar and a sweep of a forepaw that would have ripped out the ribs of the filly if it had landed.

That taught her that there is nothing so small and so harmless that it may be treated with careless cruelty. Not that this was a moral lesson with Dark Rosaleen. For since that first lesson in pain on the moonlit night in the gorge, she had been attempting to pay back to the world all of the suffering which it had given her.

If the adventure with the mother grizzly did not teach her gentleness, it taught her profound caution. It was because of the first lesson, indeed, that she was able to live through the second, which was a hundred times more dangerous.

She had grazed into a corner of a great field where the barbed-wire fences joined at an oblique angle. The hillside ran up sheer as a cliff, well-nigh, at the one side, and from the hillside a huge oak tree leaned across the nearest fence. Among the leaves a mountain lion had stretched its tawny length upon the thickest branch.

Above all other titbits in the world, a puma loves horse meat.

Dark Rosaleen had roamed in a delightful languor until the fence barred her way to the hilltop, and there she paused, her breast close to the barbs. She knew them of old. Every range horse does.

Then, as she stood there, a sudden horror prickled down her back; that same voice from the other world which had warned her of the grizzly's rush made her toss her head up, and she saw the flying peril already in the air. She saw the spread of cruel talons. She saw the great mouth gaping. And all that nightmare vision hurled toward her.

She dropped cowering, and as she shrank the monster shot across her back, missed the neck, at which he had aimed claws and teeth, and crashed full into the fence. The taut wires flung him back, gashed, half stunned and mad with rage.

Dark Rosaleen was neatly trapped. She stood in the very fork of the fence and if she strove to retreat she would be running into the claws of the destroyer. Even so, she was swerving to run the hopeless gantlet when the great cat screamed. And it drove the filly into a madness of fear. The fence was flush before her. But she barely saw it. She reared, launched herself forward—and behold, the dreadful wire did no more than nick one hind hoof as she flew across to safety.

The round-up, when it came, was an unforgettable day in the life of the filly. It was her

119

second encounter with men, the first having been the roping in the gorge that night of nights when the master was driven from her. For what she had learned of Lupin, and from him, she set carefully to one side in her wise young mind. And though in scent and in voice and in appearance he was like others of the species, there were things which set him apart—all those things for which she had mourned so bitterly after he was first away. The others, without exception, were brutes more terrible than grizzlies and mountain lions, for whereas the beasts of prey struck and killed with little pain, men came near only to inflict suffering and then passed on, leaving the savage rankling memory behind them. At least they did not capture her easily on the round-up day. Three men and six horses were worn out on the first day's run, chasing a phantom as elusive as the morning mist. When they passed her too close she made for a fence, floated over it and danced across the next field, or turned to eye them with contempt while they cut through the wires and followed hotly after her.

So, on the second day, Jerry Flynn himself went out, and they brought her into the herd of the other horses after five hours of heartbreaking work.

But old Flynn swore that she would be worth it tenfold when she grew up. With the rest she was brought into the big corrals, and then the yearlings were dexterously sifted from the others, roped and dragged to the branding. It was not the pain that tormented Dark Rosaleen most when her turn came. It was the terrible sense of calamity about to fall upon her before the actual branding. It was the scent of smoking hair and hide which came chokingly into her nostrils; it was the swirl and the flash of the leaping colts as they strove to escape the inescapable ropes; it was the relentless pressing in of the cowpunchers with the snaky lariats in their hands; and above all the deep, stern, cruel voices of the men as they worked and cursed.

She rose from that torture with an L inside a circle burned into her shoulder, and when she was loosed she ran like a mad thing for half an hour until she was alone again among the hills. Man had touched her again, defiled her, crushed her, and there was no way in which she could tell him of her hatred. But she knew now, that it was folly to run with the herd and that she never would be asked to run with it unless there was harm for her at the end of the day. Before the summer passed she had become that rare creature—a lone horse, living and feeding and playing alone, just as a wolf will sometimes separate from his fellows and make his kills singly. She came to know the range, every watercourse and every water hole, the groves, the blow sands, the bits of richest pasture. The result was that when the naked autumn came to an end and the other horses grew thin, Dark Rosaleen was shining sleek and round.

It was as savage a winter as her first had been mild. The whole caviya was brought in to be sheltered in the sheds and corrals and fed a scant portion of hay; but they could not bring in Dark Rosaleen. They chased her for three days this time, but it was like trying to catch an eagle. She would hide like a rabbit in a bush; she would mix her trail like a cunning old fox; or she would simply breeze away from them with her matchless speed. She was hardly twenty months old, but she could laugh at the fastest thing on four hoofs that the ranch possessed, even when it was un-saddled—how complete was her superiority when the pursuing horses were burdened with riders!

"Let her stay out," said old Jerry Flynn. "This here winter will either kill her or else make her a true tough one. We'll toss a coin and take the chance; the odds are about three to one against her."

February nearly killed her, and on one day she would have died indeed if she had not pawed away a crust of snow and found beneath it a rich store of the dead grasses. That lucky find brought her into March and better weather. And when the rest of the caviya was brought out in April, the ribs of Dark Rosaleen were barely showing. Jerry Flynn had gone out half a dozen times through the winter and examined her from the distance with his glasses; for he could hardly get within rifle shot of the vixen. And when the spring rolled over the mountains, painting them green, and the filly stepped out of the colt days into her maidenhood, he freely advertised the news that upon his ranch walked the winner of the great Comanche Cup two years hence.

"It's the wild life that's making her," said Jerry Flynn, "and she ain't going to have nothing else—not a strap on her till she's a four-year-old. But when she starts through Comanche Pass that fall, heaven help them that tries to foller her!"

Curious neighbors, ranchers and cowpunchers rode over on Sundays and hunted for hours to find her. The lucky ones who caught a glimpse or perhaps were able to study her for a moment through their glasses reported to their fellows that she was a beauty. She stood her full height now, which was half an inch under sixteen hands and, though there was something to be wished in the way of substance, she was growing fast in bulk and there was plenty of bone to build on; but that spring, some men thought afterward, was the very height and heyday of her beauty—just as some girls of sixteen are lovelier than ever before or since.

The next winter was a stern one also, but Dark Rosaleen had learned how to bid defiance to cold and scant provision before this. Whereas the other horses liked to feed as close as possible to the water holes, water once in two days would keep Dark Rosaleen in a pinch. She could withstand a blizzard in winter and a dust storm in summer; and when even the range cows, leather-tough and wise as Satan, grew weak and went down in the late winter, Dark Rosaleen was flourishing.

She became a great thief. She used to stand on bleak hills and watch the rich feed thrown out to the others in the corrals while the wind where she stood was cutting her to the vitals. Then, knowing that the ranch buildings were the source of an inexhaustible supply of delicacies, she used to come down on pillaging expeditions in the middle of the night when all good horses were long since fast asleep. The fences were mere trifles to such a jumper as Dark Rosaleen. She could hop over six feet of bars with ease, and a seven-foot fence was a mere frolic to her.

Rosaleen could locate a door in an instant, and then she would work at either side of it. When her strong teeth had a hold it was a stout staple indeed which could refuse to give way. Many a wooden latch she broke before she learned how to lift them. And what treats were within! Hay and oats and crushed barley, a lesser delicacy, and even the straw of the barn was far better than nothing. She was wild enough to know better than to eat too much, which a domesticated work horse will always do. Had her wits been dulled by constant manhandling, she would have been foundered on her first plunder expedition.

So Dark Rosaleen laughed her way through the winter and in the spring that followed turned the day of her fourth birthday; and Jerry Flynn decided to catch her up and bring her in.

Men still talk of that chase. They worked like furies for a week. The pick of the county came on their fastest horses—John Seaton came on Sir Gilbert, the fleet and hardy bay which had won the Comanche Cup the year before and was the favorite to win again. Peter Mince came on his beautiful black, Lofty. Others dropped in, partly to help catch the artful filly and partly because they wished to see this great contender for the Comanche Cup. But they could not put a rope on her until finally they had built a barrier across a cut through the hills where she often ran to evade them. So they trapped her; and when she found her way was blocked, she turned and charged straight back on them like a mad thing! She struck Charlie Patten, knocking him to the ground. Then half a dozen ropes settled on her and she was taken.

One wild, brief struggle, and then Dark Rosaleen submitted. She knew of old that the strength of a rope cannot be fought against; she allowed herself to be led meekly back to the home corral while the crowd followed, wondering. But her meekness of manner did not deceive them; her soul shone in her big eyes and that soul spelt mischief.

"What that horse needs is gentling, not breaking," said John Seaton.

"D'you want the job?" asked Jerry Flynn. And when there was no answer he added: "I been ranching, man and boy, these fifty years. I've never seen a hoss that couldn't be busted. Dark Rosaleen ain't going to be no different. She'll pitch some, maybe, but I got them that can ride her!"

"Them that could ride her" were Joe Masters and Chuck Lorraine, two bronc busters of repute. These experts snubbed the nose of Dark Rosaleen to the horn of a calm old cow pony's saddle and cinched a saddle on the filly. But there was no need of a blindfold or of any of the usual precautions. She did not plunge or struggle as an ordinary horse will do. But there was something more terrible still about Dark Rosaleen, something far worse than a squealing, kicking, mad-eyed mustang. For there was no more movement to her than an occasional tensing which made the ropelike muscles of shoulders and haunch stand out and quiver for an instant. Her body was strong enough to drag a plow through stiff ground; but all that it would be required to do was to lash those slender legs through the air. No wonder that she could gallop like the wind.

"She's a beauty," said Charlie Patten. "Every bit of her is meant for use! Feel her!"

And he pushed his thumb into her flank; she was hard as iron. What gave her the sleekness was not fat but a sheathing of tough muscle. And as she waited for the crisis which was to come, she looked from one man's face to another. Indeed, it seemed that she was writing those faces down in her memory.

"She'll be an old hoss before I come behind her heels!" said Jerry Flynn. "A hellion—that's what she is!"

But when Joe Masters sat in the saddle and the old cow pony was led clear, Dark Rosaleen merely drew a great breath, so that Joe's knees bulged out on either side.

"Tickle her with the spurs and see if you can get some action, Joe!" suggested a wag.

Joe turned his eyes but not his face to the speaker. He was white about the puckered mouth.

"She's just laying her plans," said Jerry Flynn. "Pretty soon Joe will have his party."

The mind of Dark Rosaleen was filled with two things—the one was a grim expectation of an agony about to come upon her at the hands of this creature who now sat upon her back; the other was the contemplation of the bit between her teeth. She took a step; she looked around her. She was the center of a widespread circle of mounted men, all with noosed ropes ready in their hands.

A voice spoke to her. It came from the man

in the saddle, a husky, strained voice, and suddenly the mare knew that the rider feared her. The iron chain bit into her jawbones.

With that, she dropped flat and rolled. An excited shout from the ring, the rider jumped clear, and as she heaved to her feet again he was once more in the saddle. Dark Rosaleen went on up into the air as though she were going over an eight-foot fence. When she landed it was upon stiffened forelegs, and from the back corners of her eyes she saw the head of Joe Masters snap down against his chest as though he had been struck with a club. At the same time the iron hand seized her jaw, the bit wrenched down and her mouth was torn open. It was keen torture.

She leaped again and as she landed Joe Masters was flung like lead to the ground.

A long-spurred burr was clinging to the toe of his boot. Joe picked it off and coming to the mare he inserted it under her saddle blanket. Now let Chuck do his best! What happened thereafter every man present would never forget. When poor Chuck settled in the saddle, Dark Rosaleen went off like a rocket and exploded in midair.

She did not cling to the pure style of sun-fishing, but combined fence-rowing and sun-fishing and half a dozen other methods in thirty seconds of madness, at the end of which Chuck sailed out of the saddle and landed on his head in the dust.

Jerry Flynn offered no less than $500 to the man who could stay three minutes on the back of Dark Rosaleen. That offer stood a month and the money was never claimed, but it cost some twenty hardy aspirants a sum total of six broken legs, as many shattered collar bones and sundry cracked ribs. At the end of the fourth week Jerry Flynn sold Dark Rosaleen to the organizers of a midsummer rodeo for a box of cheap cigars.

And on the last day of the rodeo Doc Thompson turned Dark Rosaleen against the best in the country with a prize of a round thousand dollars if anyone could ride her out.

Three men more heroic than wise swung into the saddle on the mare that day, and three men rolled in the dust before one full minute had elapsed.

Doc Thompson auctioned her off after the rodeo had closed. Someone offered two dollars for her hide.

"Are there any more bids?" asked Doc Thompson. "I'm offered two dollars for the hide of Dark Rosaleen. Is there anyone who'll bid on the horse inside the skin? Going, gentlemen, going, going, to Mr. Skinny Murphy, and now I sell her—"

A voice spoke from the ring.

"I'll offer a hundred, Mr. Thompson."

The auctioneer turned with a whimsical smile beginning on his lips, but when he saw the speaker, the smile vanished.

"Pardon me, Colonel Savary," said Doc Thompson. "I suppose you're having a joke with us?"

"Were you or were you not," said the colonel, "about to sell the mare to Mr. Murphy, who would kill her and take her hide?"

"It seems a hard thing, I guess, to a hoss lover like you, Colonel Savary," said Doc Thompson. "But what sort of use could anybody put Dark Rosaleen to?"

"One could turn her loose in the pasture and enjoy her beauty."

If another man had said such a thing the crowd might have chuckled, but it was too widely known that Colonel Savary was a ruined man and that the cause of his ruin had been the expense of breeding horses. For the sake of his horses he had crushed his fine ranch with a burden of mortgages; for the sake of his horses, men said, he had broken the heart of his wife and seen her wither and die; for the sake of his horses lovely Nell Savary was dressed like a ragged orphan.

Those keen-eyed, hard-faced cattlemen looked upon him with awe and with gentleness. There was not a man among them who would not have delved into his bank account to help the colonel, but each one would rather have faced a desperado's gun than the eye of the colonel when charity was offered to him.

"Is she mine?" he asked.

"Not at that price. She's yours for ten dollars, colonel, and I feel as if eight of those were a gift to me."

"Mr. Thompson," said the colonel, "it is an insult to horseflesh to buy such an animal for less than a hundred dollars. If there is a devil in her, I pity her for it and I blame the inhuman brutes who put that spirit in her!"

Nell had her mother's slender grace and beauty, but was enough like her father to possess a clue to the workings of his mind, and if it had not been a time of crushing poverty, this would have been the smoothest period of the colonel's life. Yet, because Nell could be as silent as he, he was perhaps a little afraid of her. He even hesitated an instant at the door, this day, before he went inside; and the first thing he saw was the faded blue of the dress she wore. What would a hundred dollars do for her wardrobe? But, as was his habit, he brought out the disagreeable truth at once.

"Nell," he said, "I've found a horse. Picked up a bargain for a hundred."

"Yes, we need one to fill out the second span. Then the work can start with the four-horse plow on that bottom land—"

"Plow horse? No, no, Nell. I've bought Dark Rosaleen."

There was a pause, and the eyes of his daughter considered him very gravely.

Then Nell turned her face away.

"It isn't true," she whispered to herself. "He hasn't done such a cruel, selfish thing. I won't believe it, I won't!"

And she went out to see. She came panting around the corner of the barn, and there, behind the eight-and-a-half-foot fence of the breaking corral stood Dark Rosaleen. Nell cried out in wonder and admiration.

She saw Dark Rosaleen turn her head at the sound and flatten her ears. It gave her instantly a snaky look of incredible malice, and Nell paused with a shudder. But there was something in the beauty of the head and in the strong slender legs which made her sigh: "Poor Sally June—poor Sally!"

She was aware of a shadow behind her and turned to face Sheriff Carey.

"I heard about the colonel having the mare," he said, "and I've come along to take a look at her."

"Why," she said, "I understood that you used to go to the Flynn place once a month to take a look at her?"

"I've never seen her too often," replied the sheriff. "Ain't she a ripsnorter, Nell?"

"If she were in the Comanche Race!" murmured the girl.

He began to untie his cinches.

"Are you staying with us a while?" she asked him.

"I'm going to be hanging around for a time," said the sheriff blandly. "Lupin has busted loose ag'in, and I'm aiming to collect that thousand dollars that they've offered for him."

"And you think he'll come straight back to her once he gets from the prison?"

"I wouldn't bet more'n ten to one."

There was no scrap of meat in the house except a bit of bacon, and what she finally offered to her father and the self-invited guest was a few strips of the bacon, some pone and black coffee. To the colonel it seemed to make no difference; he always ate what was placed before him without comment and at the table

134

he rarely made an effort to converse. The sheriff was a silent man also, after his first outbreak of words when he reached the ranch that evening. And between them Nell was utterly wretched. She did her own share as valiantly as she could, but the conversation fell away to nothing; they finished the miserable meal in silence, and then the sheriff sat on the veranda with the rancher. Nell, as she washed the dishes, stepped curiously into the hall now and again, but there was never a word spoken between the two. She stole out through the screen door and looked at them. Each was smoking a pipe, and the pulsing glow of the tobacco faintly lighted their faces, then lost them again in gloom.

She went back to her work, and when she had finished it and stepped out onto the veranda the sheriff had gone and her father was still smoking as peacefully as the night. The old feeling of helplessness swallowed Nell. What she prayed for most of all was such self-control that she would never break out against her father and declare in fierce words that his dignity was half shiftlessness, his quiet was half laziness. For, apart from other reasons, she felt that he could never understand. He had grown calloused in his part; for to put a guest at such a supper table two years before

135

would have been an agony to him, but now it was not a riffle on the smooth surface of his mind.

She went hastily back into the house, for though, as the screen door closed behind her, the thick and sultry air of the indoors rolled at her from the floor, it was better to be in the shadow where she could remain alone. She stood a long time in that hallway, silent, until she heard a faint sound of a breath drawn so suddenly deep that it was like a groan. And it struck a horror through Nell, for it told her—how much more than words!—that the suffering of the colonel had been great indeed that night.

She went up to her room, and there she sat a long time, reproaching herself for the smallness of her soul, until she heard the slow and heavy step of her father mount the stairway and enter his bedroom. His bed creaked at last, the house was still, and through the window a ray of moonshine glided. She knew then that there was no sleep for her on this night of misery, so she went softly into the hall and down the stairs. At the first landing she paused, for she had heard a sound behind her like a foot upon the carpet.

All that she could see, however, was a wall of blackness, and she stole on soundlessly.

Yet, as she reached the level of the hall beneath, it seemed to Nell that she heard the same sound again, and then a faint creak of the woodwork stopped her heart. Beyond a shade of doubt someone was coming down the steps and it could not be her father!

She flattened herself against a recess in the wall and waited until her straining eyes saw a dim outline grow out of the dark above her and pass into the faintly distinguishable form of a man. He stepped into the hall, went by her, and then hung in midstride as though an extra sense had apprised him of danger. Half a second he stood there, then whirled and cold metal was thrust under her chin; she felt the round muzzle of a revolver against her throat.

"I'll shoot if you make a sound," whispered the prowler. A hand closed on the upper part of her arm. "A woman!" murmured the man with the gun, and half of her terror dropped away from her.

The gun was withdrawn.

"Walk down the hall to the door," she was commanded. And she went cautiously, guarding the sound of her footfall.

"Go outside."

She obeyed again, and he followed her; even that noisy screen door, under his skillful touch, made not a sound.

They stood in the thick, steep shadow which fell from the roof over the veranda, but enough moonlight entered to show her a man of middle height with wide shoulders and long arms. He had put away his gun.

"Look here," he told her, "I don't want to harm you, but I have to be sure that you won't harm me. I have a job on my hands."

It was Lupin; she knew it suddenly and surely, and the last of her fear dissolved, for how can fear and pity live together? It was poor Mark Lupin, and his "job" would be to try to steal away Dark Rosaleen. It was not hard for her to make up her mind on whose side she would stand.

"You're Mark Lupin. The sheriff told me you would come."

"Carey?"

"Yes."

"What made him guess it?"

"He knew that you'd come back to Rosaleen."

"Where is he?"

"Waiting for you; near Dark Rosaleen, I imagine."

He slumped suddenly against the wall of the house with a faint groan.

"What'll I do?" he whispered to himself. "Carey was an old man four years ago!"

"Why were you in the house?"

"I've been waiting there since last night—in the attic."

"You haven't eaten."

"I don't need food. I need the horse!"

"I can give you bread and milk in the kitchen. Will you come? Besides, I have things to tell you about the mare."

"What things?" he demanded fiercely. "She's sound and whole?"

"I'll tell you while you eat."

She turned back into the house without waiting for his permission, and when she stood in the kitchen he was behind her. There she lighted a candle, as throwing less light, and turned up a pan behind it to cut the glow away from the window. Then she mixed a great bowl of bread and milk and placed it before him. He ate wolfishly, sitting upon one corner of a chair half turned away from her as though for secrecy, and yet with a constant outlook upon her from the corner of a pale blue eye. A shapeless black felt hat was jerked low over his forehead; his cheeks were drawn and of the prison pallor; he was so thin that three things stood in high relief—the jutting jaw, the high cheek bones and the gleam of his eyes. She noticed the long and agile fingers, blunted at the tips from the prison labor.

And he bolted the food ravenously, cautiously, more like a wolf than a man. If she had lost her fear of him when they stood in the dark, it rushed back over her now that she could see him. He was as dangerous, as remorseless as a wild beast.

"Talk!" he commanded, pausing suddenly.

"What's there to say about her?"

"How did you know she was here?"

"I slid into town last night and heard a bit of talk while I was outside a kitchen—that the mare from Jerry Flynn's place belonged to Colonel Savary now."

"They tried to break her while you were away, but they couldn't. No man has ever been able to ride her."

He pushed the bowl away.

"She's waited for me to come back to her," he said. "I'll ride her."

"Do you really think that she can remember?" Nell asked gently, and her very gentleness made him realize what strong arguments could not have done. He shrank back in the chair, and one of his hands slipped off his knee and hung dangling toward the floor.

"She used to understand when I talked to her. How can you get around that? I didn't need to talk. She used to read my face! She used to read my mind, I tell you!"

The tears sprang into the eyes of Nell Savary. He began to argue; it was rather pleading than arguing.

"It's only four years," he said. "Heaven above, is that very long to remember, after we had been pals together? What do you say to that? Isn't it logical?"

Her lips were trembling and she could only whisper, "I wish it were! Oh, I wish it were!"

"There'll be no harm in trying," he said finally.

"But Newton Carey is watching near the corral. Have you forgotten? You mustn't go!"

He stood up.

"What makes you care?" he asked her.

"I've known horses too. And I've lost one, too, that I loved."

He nodded, then he jerked the door open and was instantly outside, and Nell waited for the sound of his steps to pass away, for the ground was covered with thick dead grass that crackled like paper. She heard not so much as a whisper, but when she went to the door in turn and looked out, wondering why he was waiting, he was not there. He had quite vanished, and the heart of Nell leaped, though whether it was more in fear or in excitement she herself was unable to tell.

She turned back into the kitchen to extinguish the candle. Then she hurried outdoors. She went by the front way, for no matter how Lupin had been able to pass through the grass without setting up a rustling noise, she knew that she could not succeed; so she stole around through the yard in front of the old ranch house and back toward the barns and the corrals. She found no trace of Lupin; but almost immediately she caught sight of the sheriff. He lay full length in the black shadow raised by a dense growth of bushes at a little distance from the small breaking corral in which Dark Rosaleen was still pacing restlessly back and forth, back and forth, with her head turned ever toward the shadowy and distant mountains. In easy range of this spot the wise old sheriff was the more perfectly sheltered from all observation by the very rising of the moon which, though it made all else almost as bright as the sun, yet made the shadows thicker and blacker than ever. And the sheriff might have remained there in the most perfect security had it not been for a single flaw in his perfect shelter; and like the vulnerable point of Achilles, it was at the heel.

A single small ray of light glided through the bank of shrubbery and fell, alas, straight upon the bright and new-polished spur! It was a point which the most casual eyes would have caught upon instantly; no sooner had she come around the house than Nell noticed it. How could that eye of Lupin's, animal in alertness, fail to make out the sheriff, guiding his eye from that single bright point to the dull and sprawling outlines of the form along the ground?

Out of the gloom behind the sheriff a singular figure rose, which she thought for an instant was a beast; it dissolved into the form of a man going upon hands and knees, and now it flew through the air and struck the sheriff. There was neither struggle nor outcry.

Lupin rose, drawing up a limp thing with him. He carried the collapsed form of the sheriff into the moonlight and trussed him with twine. Hands and feet were bound with wonderful rapidity, and then a handkerchief was wadded and thrust into his mouth.

He did not stop there to gloat over his victory, but he whirled at once and advanced straight upon Dark Rosaleen, who had stopped in the midst of her pacing and had eyed with sharply pricked ears the skirmish among the shadows outside the corral. Then, with his breast against the upper bar of the fence, he stretched his arms to her and called:

"Whist, honey! I've come back to you!"

The heart of Nell Savary stopped, for the

mare had stepped forward a half pace. It was four long years, all the time between colthood and maturity. How *could* she remember? And, indeed, it seemed she did not.

Dark Rosaleen, out of her slow advance, leaped forward like a thunderbolt with her head darting out like the head of a snake and her mouth gaping. The teeth clashed a fraction of an inch from the face of Lupin as he recoiled: the fence timbers groaned as she crashed against them, and then she went raging around the corral, striking at the air with her fore hoofs, kicking imaginary enemies, shaking her head and gnashing her teeth—the very fury of a wicked spirit which has missed its kill. The dust which she had raised in a cloud finally blew away and revealed her standing sullenly, head down, her rump turned toward Lupin, as though she were resolved not to pay any further attention to the man she had so nearly destroyed.

And Mark Lupin? Like a madman he had actually stooped through the bars and was now standing unprotected within the corral.

Even to the fierce mare that strange and daring act came as a surprise. With one ear flattened and one canted forward she looked from the back corners of her eyes and watched him; there was even a beginning of fear in her, though he was unarmed save the thing which alone gave her fear of men, and that was the coiling shadow of a rope in his hand. She considered for half a second; then Lupin made a step toward her, and the furious hate of Dark Rosaleen set her in motion. It was not for nothing that her flanks had been scored by the spurs of strangers, her sides burned with whips, and her throat half choked by the straining nooses of lariats; whenever they came near her it was a torment, and she waited hungrily from day to day for a chance to repay a tithe of what she had endured. She let her weight fall back upon her hind quarters, then swung sharply about with her heels as a pivot and lunged again at Lupin. No retreat, however swift, could save him now and to dodge the plunge of Dark Rosaleen was beyond imagining.

Lupin was not even attempting to stir but stood bolt upright as though trying to quell her with the power of his eye.

He had thrown up his hand—like a straw against the lifted front of a wave—and now he whistled between his teeth to her. And that sound entered into the brain of Dark Rosaleen. Somewhere in the past she had known the sound. It cut through her savagery for a breathing space, and so she veered at the last instant and shot past Lupin, leaving him unharmed.

To the farther side of the corral she swung, and there faced him. Behold, Lupin was walking straight upon her, with his hand outstretched; walking very slowly and there was neither steel nor leather nor rope across his palm!

A barrier was torn away in her inward being. Fear departed from her, and her rage faded. She lowered her head and sniffed cautiously at the extended hand; she began to listen to a softly murmuring voice.

When Lupin turned and walked away, Dark Rosaleen walked at his heels!

But these wonders were not enough. He passed into the barn, and Dark Rosaleen began trotting up and down the side of the corral from which he had stepped, whinnying, first softly with impatience, and then a wild, ringing note of anxiety. It brought Lupin hurrying from the barn with saddle and bridle. And so he unbarred the entrance to the enclosure and let Dark Rosaleen come freely forth.

She was away like an arrow off the string. Was she gone forever, running straight for those mountains which she loved; and had Lupin indeed thrown away a treasure beyond price? No, no; the hoofs beat softly on the sand as she wheeled back. She careered through the moonshine in the exuberance of her joy, not at freedom, but at the knowledge that her master had returned to her!

Dark Rosaleen was standing while the heavy saddle was thrown across her back; she was merely twisting her head around to examine the busy hands of Lupin as he drew the cinches tight and tied the straps. She opened her mouth to admit the bit of the bridle; and now Lupin swung into the saddle.

As a rule she had started to pitch off saddle and rider before the torment of spur could have a chance to start, but now she merely straightened again with a little shudder, and then floated away at a gallop, heading north for the shadows of the great mountains.

An immense loneliness came over Nell. She turned sadly away and found herself confronting Sheriff Newton Carey, with the twine which had bound him dangling from one hand and the revolver in his other, and an absentminded look upon his face.

"Mr. Carey!" she cried at him. "You watched him ride away—you didn't lift a hand—"

"Nell," he said, "If you tell this on me, they'll laugh me to death and out of office. But what could I do? He could have punched

147

a hole in me and tied in a ticket to kingdom come. But now that he has a fair start, I'll give him the running of his life!"

Indeed, the sheriff did his utmost to cling to the trail of Lupin, but it was like trying to follow a dark star through infinity. He changed horses and rode for thirty-six hours, only to find that the will-o'-the-wisp had floated over the mountains.

The sheriff's repute would have been ruined, had not the price on the head of Lupin been doubled, and the doubling brought out three separate posses, the men of which labored hotly through the mountain trails, and closed their hands on thin air. So that instead of pointing a finger of scorn at the sheriff, men had to admit that Newton Carey could not perform the impossible.

Lupin had found a pleasant retreat among a tangle of little mountain streams. It was ten days before his flour gave out and he dropped down toward the lowlands for a new supply. That evening he was jogging comfortably when he came on a sight that brought him up sharply as the crack of a gun. It was a fine gray gelding in a bit of rich pasture, and on the hip of the horse the brand was a cross with a half moon stamped above it, inverted. That brand was the one which had appeared on the hip of the mare which gave birth to Dark Rosaleen and died in the desert; and he who owned the gray no doubt owned Dark Rosaleen as well, if his rights were given to him.

Lupin went on again in a melancholy humor; she had been so utterly his own and only his in the past month that he had forgotten another might have even a claim upon her. When he saw the wavering smoke of a camp fire, he could not avoid the temptation to go to it.

He rode into the circle of the firelight, and from the other side of the fire a bulky old man squinted across at him. Half a dozen rusted traps lay near him. The trapper greeted the stranger with a voice of the heartiest welcome.

"Hello, Lupin," he said, "you happened in just right for supper. Sit down."

Lupin asked how he was recognized.

"By Dark Rosaleen, what else?"

"Do you know this area well?" asked Lupin.

"I do," said the trapper.

"Who owns the ranch about five miles back—the one with the cross and semicircle for a brand. I saw it on a big gray gelding. A fine big horse about sixteen hands, with black points."

"I know that hoss. A fine set-up one, too, but that's because Colonel Savary bred him; and he's got a pint of that Savary's Arab blood in him. Savary raised that hoss, and it's Savary's brand."

The heart of the fugitive turned to ice. He remembered, again, how the hand of poverty had showed in the house of Colonel Savary. And he remembered, too, the sad, earnest eyes of the girl. They looked suddenly and intimately into his mind.

"That gray was the last hoss that the colonel run in the race for the cup. That was the last fine hoss that he could afford to keep. Right after that he went bust and sold out pretty near everything to keep a house over his head. But I seen the race run, and I seen the gray come smashing in right on the heels of the Tolliver stallion. Dog-gone me if it wasn't close, and over a twenty-five-mile stretch too!"

The words of the trapper misted together in the mind of Lupin; only vaguely he heard the story of the great endeavors of the rancher and how his fortunes had crumpled under the strain.

"And it was a hound of a yaller dog that

busted him up twice when he had a chance to do something. It was Sam Toomey that done it. He ruined that fine mare, Sally June, when the Comanche Cup running was just around the corner and Sally was sure the best of the lot; then he stole Sally when she was about to have a colt that might have been as good as her. Well, Lupin, if ever a man had hard luck, it was old Colonel Savary. He sent to Arabia for the mare that started his breed. He paid the cost of three hosses. All fine mares. One of em' died on the ship of a fever. One got spoiled in an accident. And the one mare that was left only lived long enough to leave behind her two foals. When Sally June was stole they say that it turned him a bit crazed but he never whimpered."

"What became of Sally June?" asked Lupin hoarsely.

Nell had used that gentle name.

"A storm blowed up and Toomey rode for his life and left the hoss behind him in the desert. She must of got down and been covered with a drift of the sand."

Thirty-five horses were gathered to race for the Comanche Cup; not that more than a dozen were expected to make the real running for the prize, but every large cattle owner in the country took pride in putting forward the best horse and best rider he could furnish. There was a five-hundred-dollar entrance fee required, then proof that the horse was foaled and raised in the county, and after that it was permitted to run, so long as it ran in the name of a man resident in that section of the range.

These had seemed considerable restrictions, at first, but the number of entrants grew every year. The most close-fisted and hard-headed of the ranchers began to see a type of horse evolving which was consummately useful on the range to work the cattle—a fleet, hardy, intelligent animal which could take care of itself and its rider in bad ground or weather. They came into the lists one by one. They opened their checkbooks and gave something to be added to the prize for the year. Men remembered the Comanche Cup in their wills, and at the same time that they gave five hundred to one charity and five hundred to another, they were apt to slip in five hundred more for the cup. Every year had swelled its value until the winning for this season would bring to the lucky man not only that most prized privilege of writing his name upon the cup of gold, but he would also pocket a full $30,000 in greenbacks.

It was a stake worthy of ranking with the

great events of the Eastern racing season, but no reporters came to watch its running; it was as far from publicity as it was from big cities, and having made the running of the cup strictly a county affair, the world outside of the county refused to pay any heed to it.

The start was at high noon, at which time Mr. Josiah Camden would fire a revolver into the air and Sheriff Newton Carey would see that the start was even. If not, the horses would be brought back and sent away again up the steep incline of the floor of the valley. The steepness of the shadows announced that the very instant of noon was drawing closer and closer; and the horses began to be ridden from the shadows of the trees, where they had been resting, and brought to the starting point; nearly three dozen sleek, well-trained horses, and three dozen anxious riders. The riding of the Comanche Pass at any time was hazardous and at high speed it was a murderous test.

But there was only a small group to watch the start. Hardly a dozen were assembled to look on; though there were many hundreds who came to watch the running each year, these posted themselves at places of vantage among the peaks where they could overlook considerable sections of the Pass itself and see the varying degrees of daring with which the riders pushed their horses from one danger to another. A still larger number were assembled to see the finish near the town of Las Gatas, twenty-five miles away. There stood the golden cup; and at the finish, also, the prize money was waiting.

However, what the little group at the start lacked in numbers it made up in enthusiasm. The line was marked; the horses were gathered in a straightened string; and the silence lay heavily in the valley waiting for the starter's gun, when a voice cried out of the sky, so it seemed. Looking up bewildered, they saw Dark Rosaleen dancing down the clifflike face of the slope above them. She weaved from side to side, bouncing from foothold to foothold, and once they drew in their breath with a universal groan as she slipped a dozen feet and started a cataract of pebbles and stones rattling down the declivity before her. But without another accident she came smoothly to the foot of the slope, and they found Mark Lupin sitting the saddle in their midst. He looked about him as calmly as though Sheriff Carey were not a dozen feet away with his gun in hand.

"I've come to enter Dark Rosaleen," he said to them, "in the name of Colonel Savary.

Am I here in time?"

He looked about him with a smile which was rather stern than mirthful. "I was delayed getting the entrance money."

And he held out a wallet packed fat with greenbacks, waiting for it to be taken by the proper man. The sheriff came reluctantly to the front.

"You've made yourself my prisoner, Lupin," he told the man on Dark Rosaleen.

"But you've put me on parole," answered Lupin. "You've put me on parole for the running of this race!"

"Do you think I'm a madman, Lupin?"

"Not a bit; you have enough sense to know that after twenty-five miles at full speed over those mountains, even Dark Rosaleen will have no running left in her."

"Suppose you fail to finish?"

"Why am I here, then; for a joke, sheriff? If I run away, at least you're five hundred richer than you were before I came. Do you take a chance with me, Carey?"

"Tell us first your proof that Dark Rosaleen was born in this county out of a county mare?"

The whole story took only three minutes in the telling, but in the first ten seconds every man who listened rode in imagination on the top of that boxcar, covered with the red silt of the sandstorm of the night before; and then they followed each detail; they winced when Lupin rolled heavily from the top of the car and struck the ground; they winced again when his brutal foot kicked down the filly and again when he had raised the rock to dash out its life; and they followed breathlessly in the hunt for help, and they drew in their breaths with relief when they heard how the filly was fed, and how she grew stronger and played like a dog around her master every day, and how they ran, at last, into the trap in the gorge. But when he had finished his last word, and they knew how Dark Rosaleen had followed him from the corral only a short time before, they allowed a silence to come in between the finish of the story and their first speech. Then the sheriff took the wallet with a grunt and handed it to the starter.

"I say that Dark Rosaleen runs this race," said the sheriff. "If there ain't five hundred in that wallet, I'll make up the difference."

There was a short, deep-throated murmur from the crowd, but it was far more eloquent than a cheer.

"Where did you get that coin?" asked the sheriff softly beside the fugitive from justice.

"From Colonel Savary," said Lupin, and

looked the sheriff full in the eye.

The sheriff grinned.

"And what do you get out of the race, Lupin, whether you win or lose?"

"Prison," said Lupin, turning pale.

"Will you tell me, then, what in the name of heaven made you come in for it?"

Lupin stared high above him to the wide circle of a hawk which was hunting down the valley.

"I don't know, sheriff," he murmured. "I don't know what brought me in—except that the world owes something to Colonel Savary, the way I make it out."

That was all that was said before the start; then Dark Rosaleen stepped into place at one end of the line; the gun exploded and away they went in a swirl of dust. A gust of wind stooped down and tossed the dust away a minute later, and what those who stared up from the starting point saw was what had been predicted for days preceding the race—John Seaton on the big bay, Sir Gilbert, was leading the way as he had led it from start to finish the year before, but just behind him cantered the slim body of Dark Rosaleen, running, as Camden said later, "Like a river flowing, if only a river could float uphill!"

Then the last of the horses were swallowed

by the ragged throat of the Pass, and the sheriff rushed for the telephone; for a line had been strung from During to Las Gatas, the poles climbing sturdily up the rugged slopes. Every winter the line was overwhelmed with storms—covered with heaping snowdrifts and demolished with landslides. But every spring it was repaired and reerected, and on the day of the race from half a dozen posts along the route watchers cut into the line and telephoned their observations of the runners to the start and to the finish. Those reports were clear enough to the crowd at During; but to those who waited anxiously at Las Gatas there was one mystery which could not be solved.

Tony Lagrange, the cigar-store owner, stood at the window with a big megaphone clapped to his lips, and the messages which were repeated to him from the telephone he boomed out to the crowd. "They're at Grundy's Rock," thundered the megaphone. "And Seaton is leading on Sir Gilbert—"

Here a roar of applause stopped him, for Sir Gilbert had been heavily backed in the betting; a full half of the crowd had placed its money on that strong runner whose victory of the year before was fresh in all memories.

"And," boomed the megaphone, "a black

mare is following behind, going easy—going easy!"

For the sweat of her labors had turned Dark Rosaleen into a shining black by this time.

"Who is she?" asked a hundred voices.

"Must of been added at the last minute," announced the megaphone. "The mare ain't known and the rider ain't known!"

It was enough to start a heavy buzz of conversation which lasted for another twenty minutes; and where Colonel Savary and Nell sat in the buckboard under the oak tree, the colonel was making his guess as well as the others.

"It must be that black filly I saw over at Riley's place a couple of weeks back," he told Nell. "She looked fast, but she hasn't the underpinning to last out a race. She'll fade before they get halfway through the pass. That's a race for horses, not for mares!"

"Except Sally June," sighed Nell.

"Except for Sally June," he admitted gloomily, "but she was bred for work!"

The megaphone roared a second time, at last. Sir Gilbert was still leading, but behind him, fifty feet, came the black mare, still going easily, the report said. And the others were bunched quite a distance back. One horse was already out of it, and a dozen others were being plugged along without a hope of winning.

The interest had now grown hot, and when the third message indicated that positions were unchanged the whole crowd packed closely in around the megaphone to wait for further news, to make wild conjecture. But the colonel's guess had been repeated. They referred to the black mystery as Riley's mare, now.

"Ask who the rider looks like?" they pleaded.

And the answer came back: "It looks like Lupin!"

There was a roar of laughter at this crude jest. The fourth post was heard from; now it was a walkaway for Sir Gilbert. He was running even better than his race of the year before. The slender body and the meager limbs of John Seaton were a mere featherweight for that sturdy worker, and he had been put through the Pass fifty times in rehearsal; he knew every stone of the way, every climb, every descent. The rest of the contestants were now far back of Sir Gilbert. Except for the black.

What a storm rose in the little valley now! They began to offer bets thick and fast. Two to one on Sir Gilbert and one to three on the black mare. The very mystery which surrounded her was intriguing.

"When they reach the flat, Sir Gilbert will walk away from her," said the colonel with perfect surety. "They're fools to bet against that horse."

The last post in the mountains sent in the same report. As the big bay with Seaton in the saddle started to sweep down the last descent into the foothills, the rest of the horses were lost and out of view behind them, all except a slender-limbed black mare which was drifting fifty feet behind him, running easily, running easily!

In the midst of that uproar which followed the announcement the megaphone brayed again, and all were silent, sweating with excitement.

"Is Deputy Sheriff Thomas here?"

"Here!" called Thomas, and he uncoiled his gaunt length from beneath a tree and stood up, a sad-faced man with a fighting record as long as one of his prodigious arms.

"There's a message from Sheriff Carey for you."

"Let 'er rip," said the deputy, hitching his belt.

"The sheriff wants you to watch the finish,"

blared the megaphone.

Thomas chuckled.

"I ain't apt to be looking the other way," he said mildly, and the crowd laughed.

"There's a gent in that race that needs watching. It's Mark Lupin!"

The jaw of Thomas fell; and in utter silence men stared in amazement at one another.

"Listen!" thundered the megaphone. "Lupin is riding Dark Rosaleen! That must be the black mare!"

And then the storm rose, a veritable yell of wonder and excitement.

"I know what it is!" said Colonel Savary to Nell. "It's what the racing fever'll do. Lupin had rather go back to his prison if he can prove that Dark Rosaleen is better than any horse in the mountains; he's prouder of Rosaleen than his freedom. And he wants to stand in the center of the stage. Never was a crook yet that wasn't more than two-thirds child!"

"Hush!" breathed Nell, and he looked down to her in amazement.

She had raised a hand as though to ward herself from his comments and, very white of face and big of eye, she was staring fascinated at the megaphone of Tony.

"He won't finish!" she was whispering.

"He won't ride in and—and throw himself away—"

Another roar from Tony.

"Lupin has paid in the five hundred dollars; he says that Colonel Savary give it to him to enter Rosaleen."

Three thousand pairs of eyes turned in a stunned silence to gape at the colonel.

"And the sheriff says that Lupin confessed the mother of Rosaleen wore the brand of Colonel Savary. Dark Rosaleen is the colonel's hoss!"

Oh, the cheer that rose tingling then! It was like a sudden change, a happy ending in a fairy tale, but there was nothing fairylike in the white-hot sun which was beating down upon their bonnets and their sombreros, or in the white, strained face of the old colonel as he sat stiffly erect in the buckboard and drew his bushy brows down above his eyes. They swarmed about him; they wished him joy; the hundreds who had bet their last penny on Sir Gilbert cheered the old colonel.

Then the whole wave of humanity washed away to climb to the tops of the hills so that they could see the runners still far away.

"Oh, dad," cried Nell, "It's Lupin! He's giving you what belongs to you! I don't care what he's done; there's not a dishonorable drop of blood in his body."

"But the people, Nell," whispered the colonel. "I've thought that they hated me for an outlander all these years; but they cheered as though they loved me."

"They do; because they know you better than you ever knew yourself!"

She stopped, frozen with wonder, for a tear had welled out from beneath the eyelid of the colonel.

Nell stood up in the buckboard and the colonel beside her, so that they could look over the swale of the ground.

"I can't see!" breathed the colonel. "Is it—is it a close finish?"

"It's only one horse," murmured Nell.

"What's the color—in the name of heaven, Nell?"

"I can't see! It's hardly more than a speck!"

There was not long to wait, for the solitary horse was flying toward them as if the long and wearing climb through the mountains did not lie behind it. It dashed inward with the sun flashing upon its wet sides, a streak of light.

Nell strained to see. If only the sun were less blinding! Her eyes ached with staring over the whiteness of the sands. But there was only an instant more to wait. Into the valley the victor was coming, and now, far away, the beaten rider was following, lost beyond all hope. In between the hills shot the winner, galloping hard and fast. It turned a bit to dart for the finish and as it turned the sun gleamed upon the sides and brought out, for a fleeting instant, a big subdued dappling. A thousand voices thundered, "Dark Rosaleen!"

She was under the finish line. She was drawn up. She was dancing back to the crowd where the deputy sheriff stood with two guns in his hands, barking orders. But who minded the deputy? They could see nothing but this peerless beauty with one ear flattened to show her hatred for all other men; with one ear pricked to show her love for her rider.

"Did you hear?" breathed Nell at the ear of her father. "Look up and see her. She's yours, dad; your work! Oh, the beauty! Oh, *look* at her!"

The wind stooped over the roofs of the sheds and scoured across the race track and struck Bill Champion full in the face with such force that he swayed on the upper rail of the fence. He shrugged his skinny neck deeper into his coat collar, but he did not take his eyes from the big brown colt which was finishing its mile workout in the early chill of the morning.

Champion clicked the stop watch.

"One forty-one," he whispered with numb lips. "Who'd of thought that dog had it in him, and with a ton of bricks up!"

He slid the watch back into his vest pocket and flashed an angry glance around him at the weather. It was high time to be donning an overcoat, but overcoats were not numbered in his wardrobe; the last one had been pawned for the price of "snow." But since he must stay at his post in spite of all weather, he shrugged his sharp shoulders again and jerked out the morning paper. He had read the headlines; now he dived into the heart of the story.

The governor had refused to pardon Lupin; the long petition signed by the names of so many honest ranchers had gone for nothing.

The lips of Champion curled at one side and he snarled his curse; then his eye wandered on through the reporter's résumé of the strange case of Lupin and the mare. He had read it all before; but now he read it again with equal attention, for in that drug-blighted brain there was still strength enough to understand a man's love for a fine horse. He had followed the races for twenty years himself.

He put the paper away to time the next tryout, but his mind was not on his work, and

166

all the rest of that bitter autumn day he wandered about in a half dream. At night he made up his resolution and went straight to his lodging house, and there the dark chamber confirmed him; and when he stumbled on the edge of the worn carpet it seemed to Champion that it would be pleasant indeed to step away from all that life with one long stride. So he laid the gun on the table before him and wrote his note:

I killed the old man that Lupin took the fall for. I was robbing the old fool when he turned on me and I had to kill him. Lupin happened to be there, but he had nothing to do with any of it. I done the work. Now grab me for it if you can.
BILL CHAMPION

"And yet," said Nell, as they reined their horses on the top of the hill, "if Champion hadn't spoken, the truth was bound to come out some way."

Mark Lupin smiled. He was never a man to argue a point, but he rubbed the silky neck of the mare.

"After all," he said, "It was Dark Rosaleen that made him speak, God bless her! She'd bring the truth out of any man!"

Cayenne Charlie

This story appeared under the byline of
George Owen Baxter and was featured in the
February 22, 1930 issue of Street and Smith's
Western Story Magazine. Printed in that same
issue was the fourth part of a serial by Max
Brand, "Twelve Peers." (In book format, it
became *Destry Rides Again*, one of the world's
best-selling western novels.)

Thus, "Cayenne Charlie" was written when
Faust was in full stride as a prolific fictioneer
for *Western Story*. It is a unique tale in that
it offers not one but two well-character-
ized Faust protagonists: an average easterner
named Alfred Clark, who is attempting to
manage a ranch in an environment totally
alien to him, and a wild young red-haired
firebrand called "Cayenne Charlie" Bird.

Charlie is set in the mold of the mythic
Faust gunfighter, yet is presented with a lark-
ing tongue-in-cheek quality, mixing humor
and heroism.

This colorful saga of the rangeland offers a

full quota of swift shoot-and-ride action for which Max Brand is famous. The reader is catapulted into the heart of a thundering cattle stampede, struggles to cross a storm-whipped, rain-swollen river, and shares the bullet-blasted thrills of a canyon shootout.

Fred Faust at full gallop.

Consider Alfred Clark and his niece, Dinah.

Dinah: tall, strong, graceful, imperious, beautiful, and cruel.

Alfred Clark: short, weak, awkward, humble, ugly, and charitable.

She was young enough to feel that knowledge was absolute and that she had more than her share.

He was old enough to feel that knowledge is comparative and that he had not cornered the market.

She was rich in prospect and would have a million or so when she reached twenty-one.

He had been a humble, toiling lawyer all his days.

She had always been the first choice at every schoolhouse dance in the county, the first invited to every celebration, the first girl that every newcomer fell in love with, and the last he proposed to. Because, like a star, she was not only shining, but seemed distant—not in her manner, which was adapted from the ways of wild mustangs, but in herself. Men like to feel that a wife will be a possession. Nobody was apt to feel that way about Dinah.

Alfred Clark never had been retained in a big case, never had convinced an important jury, never had even so much as raised a family. He was sixty years old. He was five feet three inches tall. He hardly could begin a sentence without saying: "Excuse me."

His brother, Tom Clark, had been the exact opposite of Alfred in everything. He had been the bad boy of a bad town. And he had spent the strength of six feet of bone and muscle for thirty years without accumulating a penny. Alfred was always the good example, and Tom was always the good time.

Then Tom married a little gentle, trustful, unworldly girl who had inherited a good many thousand acres of valueless land. The land was not valueless because it was poor in quality, but because it was poor in situation and environment. That is to say, it was in a true hole-in-the-wall country populated by freehand artists with a running iron. It was a truly democratic country where a herd of cows belonged to the first comer.

Tom Clark went up into those wild highlands and brought order out of disorder. He killed three men in the first year and gathered around him for cowpunchers a gang of ex-criminals, ex-yeggs, long riders, rustlers, and jailbirds. He knew them and they understood Tom, his fists and his guns. That became a happy ranch, a busy ranch, and a ranch that turned out dollars fast enough to make the head of any man swim. But, great as he was, before his death Tom began to be known as the father of Dinah Clark.

When he lay on his deathbed—a certain brutal scoundrel had shot him full of holes, though in a fair fight—Tom Clark had named his far-off brother, Alfred, as the guardian of his daughter during the year and a half which would pass before she reached her twenty-first year. Alfred was to manage the estate, in the meantime, at a generous salary.

And manage he did! When Dinah went to a dance, Uncle Alfred also attended and sat in a corner with a bright, patient eye. She could not begin a dinner with chocolates and end it with soup. She could not go to bed at three and get up at five. She had her daily life flavored with old wives' maxims and her nights were poisoned with bad dreams. She could not speak ten words without having her grammar corrected.

However, she had her revenge. So did the punchers. The same will which made his brother the manager of the estate for a year and a half also forbade him to discharge a single member of the old crowd. The will was known to all the men, and they took advantage of it. For this unsympathetic Easterner who did not know how to use a pair of spurs or swing a rope, they shirked their work, they let the ranch run down, and when a friendly rustler appeared on the horizon, instead of blasting him into another world they winked at him askance. The great Clark herd began to diminish.

Alfred Clark talked to them in assembly. He talked to them one by one. He implored them in the name of Tom Clark. He did everything that he could. But nothing would do. He could not handle these men; but those men could handle him. They soldiered on the job, and the more they soldiered, the more Dinah smiled on them. She was what counted, in their eyes, and she wanted nothing so much as to have her uncle throw up his hands and pronounce this a bad job.

He would not do it.

Quiet, grave, gentle as a lamb; there was in him the same streak of iron that had appeared more visibly in his brother. He stuck to his guns, though they were guns of silence and reflection. If he could not stop the wagon from rolling downhill at least he could apply a brake that jarred on everyone's nerves. In the meantime, he strove to uphold and maintain the business methods of his brother.

One of Tom Clark's best moves had been to go south every year. Crossing the Mexican border, at the town of Libertad, he would gather up many hundreds of Mexican cattle, undersized, of bony backs, gaunt stomachs, and hanging heads. These he drove north, and in three months they had fattened in the rich mountain lands of the ranch where water ran in every valley and the grass was as green as a cowman could wish. These half-priced skeletons, at the end of three months, sold for nearly as much per pound, in Chicago, as the finest Durhams. They were smaller parcels, to be sure, but they had the necessary beef. This system had never failed to net him a great profit.

The trip was made by Alfred Clark, pursuing the old traditions. He had taken with him every man who could be spared for the drive home. Dinah went along also, though against his better judgment. But when he came to Libertad, the town which had loved his brother like a god looked upon him as an intruder. The prices they demanded for cattle were outrageous. It seemed for the moment that Yankee gold meant nothing to them. And Alfred Clark meant less than nothing.

When he got some cattle into the corrals, thieves broke in and took most of them.

He was in despair, and that was the reason he talked to Dinah on this night.

It was for her, after all, that he was working, except for the salary that would cover a transient year or two and then send him back to an old business newly ruined.

He sat in a chair in the corner of the room, next to a little window that looked down on the moonlight of the street. He sat quietly. He was always cool. This night beaded every brow but that of Alfred Clark. His was pale, dry, and smooth, as usual.

Dinah could not keep still. She walked up and down the room restlessly. She knew that she was in the wrong and, therefore, she was angrier and more sulky than ever.

"I've had to surrender," said Uncle Alfred.

"You mean that you're going to throw up the job," she said hopefully.

"No," he replied. "I mean that I'm failing at the work, and I've decided to ask you for your help. Do you think that you could work with me, Dinah?"

"I dunno," said she.

"Don't know," he corrected. "You blur your letters, my dear."

"Yeah?" said Dinah. "So go ahead."

"I have bought cattle every day since we came to Libertad. And a day or so after buying, most of these purchases are stolen. Our men—*your* men, really—are not providing

175

adequate protection."

"That's not my fault."

"I think it is."

"Let's have it out," said she, for she loved a fight as much as had her famous father.

"That's what I intend to do," he answered surprisingly.

"Go on, then," said the girl, squaring her jaw.

"You want me to leave," said the lawyer.

"Yes, I do!"

"I'm in the way, here."

"Yes, you are."

"Your way, and the way of the cowpunchers."

"Yes, in the way of everybody and everything!"

"But your father *wanted* me here," he said. "And with your help I could be quite effective."

"How could I help?"

"With the ranch crew. They're a bad lot."

"They were good enough for dad."

"Of course they were, because he was man enough to handle them. When they shirked, he found out why. He punished them with his fists."

"You bet he did!"

Alfred held up a puny fist and considered

it carefully.

"That's a thing I couldn't do," said he.

"Yeah," said she, "I guess you wouldn't go far down that road, Uncle Alfred."

"But you, Dinah, could easily do what I cannot do. *You* could keep the men in order. They love you for your father's sake, and for your own. They could not possibly be unfair to you, as they are to me."

"You want me to go in and handle the boys? Drop on my knees and beg 'em to be good?"

"You know the best way, if you cared to give your mind to it."

"Do I?"

"Yes, I think so."

"There's only one best way. That is for you to go back East and leave us all alone. We did pretty good before you came out. What good is wastin' all this time? Pay yourself for the year and a half, and leave."

"You mean that you definitely won't help me?"

"I dunno why I should."

"Then you have me practically beaten," said he, raising his voice a little.

"Yeah?" said the ungracious girl.

"Practically beaten, but not completely. I'm going to try for another day to find some way of solving this dilemma. If I fail, I shall step out, because it bleeds me to the heart to see my brother's estate dissipated."

"What are you gonna do?"

"Since you won't help me and I can't help myself, I shall have to look about for new levers to lift the load. It may be that I shall find them. If, at the end of twenty-four hours, I have not found the right solution, as it appears to me, I shall leave."

Her reply was broken by a great commotion on the street.

They went to the window, peered out.

They could count the bright uniforms of a dozen Mexican policemen. A crowd filled the narrow sidewalks and overflowed into the street, and down the center, accompanied by a heavily armed guard, marched a mule, with a man thrown over its back, lashed hand and foot, bound so that he could not stir. He seemed unconscious. His head dangled; his long red hair flopped with each step of the mule. As the procession passed, there were loud whoops and shouts from the crowd. Alfred Clark could hear the word "gringo," over and over again.

"It sounds as loud as a revolution, doesn't it?" asked Alfred Clark, very willing to turn the subject of conversation from the dispute.

She did not answer him, but leaning from the window she called in a voice as strong as a man's: "Hey, Harry!"

On the sidewalk beneath, a brown-faced puncher looked up to them. He was the biggest, strongest, wildest, and most troublesome of all the Clark riders. At the sight of the girl, his face broke into a grin. He waved.

"Hey, what's the big ruction?" she yelled down.

"I'll be up to tell ya!" he shouted back.

When Harry walked into the room he was big enough to fill a door—or break a hangman's rope, thought Alfred Clark. He had a low, narrow brow, with greasy black hair cataracting over it, and the line of his hatband was indented visibly around his head. His face was darkest bronze, a little shadowed in the unrazored parts. He looked like a villain.

Alfred was convinced that he was at least as bad as his looks. Yet there was no man in the world, apparently, that young Dinah Clark liked better than this brute, with his jail record, and his list of dead men!

She was smiling at him, expectantly. It seemed that the poor child had no taste in men, whatever. A fine thing if his brother's ranch should pass by marriage into the hands of this thug.

179

"Hullo, boss," said Harry, with a mere side-glance at Clark.

"Give your feet a rest, Harry," said she.

"Yeah, I don't mind."

He slumped into the most comfortable chair.

"What's up in Libertad?" Dinah asked him.

"Trouble!" said Harry.

"What kind?"

"Fists. Rough-an'-tumble. Knives. Then some guns to finish off."

"Thought I heard some shooting. Was that a dead man they were packing by?"

"Pretty near," said Harry. "I been and seen the outstandingest scrap that I ever looked at in my life."

"Let's hear about it."

"I was up to that cheap dump at the end of the street. That one with what they call a golden lion over the door. It looks a pile more to me like a sick cat." He grinned.

"Get to the story," she urged.

"Well," said Harry, "I slope into that cheap dump and look over the supply of wines and liquors, which they ain't none too fancy, and while I'm tastin' and tryin' out, preparin' for a bust as big as one dollar ninety can give, in sashays a gent with a black head of hair longer than goat's wool, and he leans on the bar and takes a look around him. He's big, this gent. You'd wanta survey him. You wouldn't wanta guess. He's got slopin' shoulders that make me feel like a boy again, and he can scratch his knees without bendin' over at all. Nobody offers him no business except the bottle, which he don't slide no change over the counter for neither. Hard-boiled. That's his first name, and the only name he's got, I reckon. But pretty soon, whacha think."

"I dunno. Gwan, Harry!" said Dinah.

"Why, pretty soon, somebody kicks the doors open, and there stands a redheaded gent that needs surveyin', too. Not for weight. He wouldn't budge no scales at more'n a hundred and seventy. But the sporting editors say that's big enough to lick the biggest. Anyway, it wasn't weight that needed the surveyin' in him. It was the nacheral fire that brimmed over in him and leaked out at his eyes." He paused for effect.

"He comes up to the bar and orders a drink. Takes a sip. Spits it out. 'This is hog wash!' says he. Then he looks down the bar an' says, 'I'll try that bottle.' And doggone me, if he don't take it out from under the nose of that black-headed bear!

"I stepped back in time to miss the fist of

181

Blackie as it shoots over the shoulder of the redhead. The whiff of it, only, was enough to make me wish that I was home in bed.

"What does the Red do? He steps in kind of easy and graceful, like he was askin' his best girl for a dance, and he soaks Blackie three times on the jaw with homemade upper-cuts, the kind that mother loved.

"Blackie goes back on his heels to think it over. Then he rocks forward with a yowl, and lets loose to plain tear Red to bits!"

"But Red didn't tear," guessed Dinah.

"That he didn't. Not hardly! He leans over and pastes Blackie four times in the face.

"Blackie, he goes crazy. He rushes in and gets a stranglehold.

"Then Red explodes. What I mean to say, they ain't no other word. He blows Blackie offen the floor, hits him five times in the air, and lands on his face when he comes down. But by this time, that bright bartender goes to the door of the shop and blows a whistle.

"When he turns around, Red is pickin' up bottles. Heaves 'em through the mirror. Crashes a pair of chairs through the windows. He scatters that crowd like a riot gun, and I wonder whether I'd better try to eat a hole through the floor, or climb up the chandelier. And all the time, mind you, Red ain't mad.

He's only enjoyin' himself.

"Then in comes the police boys, an' six of 'em go for Red. Now, he's busted the windows open, but he don't go through 'em and make a getaway. He just laughs and hollers *'Viva Méjico!'* And then he dives into that crowd. Splits it like water. Then a second wave of police come in an' *takes* Red.

"They put him down. They beat him limp. And the last thing I hear from him is: 'Been a grand ol' party, boys!' "

"Did they kill him?" cried the girl.

"Kill him?" said Harry. He leaned back in his chair and laughed so loudly that Alfred Clark gritted his teeth.

"They grab Red and sling him over the back of a mule. And it's off to jail for him. That's what you just saw goin' down the street."

"What will happen to him?"

"Aw, I dunno. Nothin' more than he can stand, anyway." And Harry laughed again. "He'll get a chance to cool off in the hoosegow."

That night, in bed, Alfred Clark lay awake with his thin arms crossed behind his head and his weary, patient eyes staring up into the darkness for a solution to his problem.

None came.

He had loved his brother with a devotion that twenty years and three thousand miles had not dimmed in the slightest, but he decided, calmly, bitterly, that he had attempted a thing that he could not carry through.

Sleep was slow in coming . . .

He breakfasted in the dining room, served by a heavy-eyed Mexican who wheezed from tobacco-choked lungs with every breath that he drew.

Breakfast over, Clark went out onto the street.

With a great uproar, a drove of cattle went past him. He watched the hollow sides, the red-stained eyes, and the long, polished horns of these animals, knowing perfectly that just such a consignment was what he needed to complete his business and start north. But he knew, also, that he never could hope to put the deal through with such men as burdened his hands.

He was a calm and patient man, but these thoughts aroused his temper until he gritted his teeth. He strolled on down the street, came to the jail.

It was part of the municipal building, built on a scale at least three or four times as great as Libertad could ever need. The liberal hand of graft appeared in its dimensions and in the cracks which seamed its walls. Clark decided that he would look into the condition of the gringo prisoner in the foreign jail.

A slattern guard with the look of a murderer listened to his request to see the white prisoner and sneered openly.

"We are busy cleaning," he said. "We have no time to waste on sightseers, señor!"

Alfred Clark grew angry, which was a rare thing with him.

"Should I have a letter of introduction?" he asked.

"Yes, señor. A letter from your president, perhaps?"

"I *have* a letter from him," said Clark, and passed a five-dollar bill into the hand of the guard.

The latter continued to sneer, partly because he had practiced that expression all his life, but he took the five dollars, pushed it into his pocket, opened the door, and gave a careless jerk of his head which invited the gringo to enter. A guard was ordered to take the visitor to the cell of the redhaired man, and let them talk for a few minutes. Five minutes would be enough.

Clark was led down the hall. There were a

185

series of rooms built with brick partitions which were quite thick, and in the face of each door was an opening screened over with steel bars.

He was directed to a small corner cell. Clark peered at the man inside, mentally listing what he saw.

Missing:

From the coat, a sleeve, and all the front buttons.

From the shirt, all buttons also, as well as the collar.

From the trousers, half of one leg.

From the feet, both boots, and most of one sock.

Added:

To the coat, several tears in a free and liberal pattern.

To the shirt, a large, greasy, black smudge across the breast, and incidental rips, together with some streaks of red.

To the trousers, the pattern which one would have expected a vigorous wild cat in the prime of life to have created.

To the face, a large purple swelling on each side of the jaw, near the point.

To the left eye, a circle of purple, relieved with cunningly worked shades and gradations of green and black.

To the right eye, one sweeping, and almost eye-closing mass, blue-black and rich to see.

To both cheekbones, large, discolored lumps.

To the nose, a swollen condition that made it as large as a pear.

The prisoner was sitting on the edge of a bunk, loaded with irons. His feet were anchored to the floor by the weight of what must have been at least a hundred pound ball of lead. Two pairs of irons were fitted about his ankles.

His arms, likewise, were confined together by two sets of handcuffs.

Yet he had managed to roll a cigarette and was now smoking it.

"Hullo, partner," said the redhead. "Look at the picture they painted on me! Then tell me what you think of it. I can only *feel* it."

"You look as though you've had a very rough time," said Clark with sympathy.

"Aw, a little stormy," said the redhead. "Nothin' much. When you get into a hurricane, you gotta expect high waves."

"I want to know how they're treating you here."

"They're treating me about average for a Mexican jail. They ain't much, you take them by and large."

"You've been in them before?"

"Yeah, I been in a few."

"Do they intend to keep you in here for long?"

"Dunno," said Red. "I don't care much what they intend to do. I'll leave when I get ready."

"You mean that you'll *escape?*" asked Clark, staring again at the irons.

"Sure," said Red. "Why not?"

"I should think those irons would be enough to keep you here."

Red laughed again. He shrugged his shoulders. "They won't hold me! I'm just restin' here an' gettin' my strength back, as you might say, and pretty soon that puffy feelin' will be out of my face. I hate to have my head all swelled up, because it makes the next bang I get so darned much more painful."

"I shouldn't ask," Alfred Clark said. "But I'd really like to know how you plan to escape."

"Well, I'll tell you," said the prisoner. "Anybody can slip handcuffs—anybody that'll practice foldin' his hands for a while, because you can make the measure around the

188

thumb and palm less'n the measure around the wrist. Just takes a little practice to get the hang of it."

"But when you've slipped the wrist irons, there are the manacles on your legs."

"Why, I just unlock those irons, when I've got my hands free."

"You don't have a key!"

"I got a key that'll fit most locks, the kind that they got in this here neck of the woods. It's a stiff bit of watch spring. I keep a snag tied in my hair close to the head, and in that snag there's the watch spring. It catches on the comb every day, but it's worth the trouble."

"I'll believe that you can do as you say and get rid of the irons, but it seems to me that you're not a great deal better off at that point, because you'll still be inside this cell. You'll have a lot of thick walls between you and freedom."

"Yeah," said Red. "But I reckon that I could pull the bricks out of that wall like blocks out of a play house. Or the bars on that door, there, would likely come out by the roots pretty easy."

"I'd like to know your name," said Clark.

"Charlie is my name. Bird is my last moniker. And Cayenne is what some puts in front of the whole job."

"Cayenne Charlie Bird?"

"That's the line up. What's your shingle say?"

"Alfred Clark. Cayenne, I'd like to talk to you—*outside* this jail. Tonight."

"That soon, eh?"

"I'm due to leave Libertad this evening." Clark hesitated. "Could you possibly break out?"

"Well, why not? Sure, I'll call at your room in the hotel."

"You will?"

"Sure."

"With the police force on your heels?"

"They'll take a while to find me."

He grinned in much enjoyment of this state of affairs, and Clark grinned also.

"Then I'll expect you at eight o'clock. There is a ten o'clock train, but I'd like to have a chat with you before I decide to take it."

"I'll be there at eight," said Red.

Little Alfred Clark walked from the jail with a shiver in the center of his spine, for he felt that he had broken the law so completely that it would never be the same again in Libertad.

By the end of that day, the head of Alfred Clark was buzzing and aching. He had been turning his thoughts for twelve hours to try to reach some solution, find some way of cutting the Gordian knot. He could not. He felt that he was foresworn if he failed to live up his contract with his dead brother. But better be foresworn than undo the work of his brother's entire life by letting the ranch go to ruin. Up to this point he had tried reason and logic. He felt that he would go still farther and try the power of sheer appeal.

Therefore, after supper, he asked to talk with Dinah alone. But she said: "It'd be a lot better if Harry came along, and one of the punchers, too. Say Buddie Vincent, eh?"

Bud Vincent was the youngest man on the place, the last to be employed by Tom Clark. He was the most insolent, outspoken, discourteous puppy that Alfred Clark had ever known. It seemed an unnecessary insult to have him present at such a conversation.

"I should think you and I could talk alone, Dinah," said he.

She looked at him with hard, sullen eyes.

"I think the men have a right to know exactly where we all stand, when we're having our last talk."

So they came up to his hotel room. It was

very hot. No wind stirred. Heat was still radiating up from the baked surface of the street and from the walls of the nearer buildings.

It was not a pleasant place for conversation. A suitcase lay on the bed. A raincoat was folded neatly on top of it, with a pair of magazines for train reading at hand. Signs of departure.

Alfred Clark could understand clearly why the girl wanted not only one but two men with her. In this company, she was fortified against him. He could not possibly break down the power of her defense. But he decided that he would shake her if he could. He struck right at the heart of the matter.

"Dinah," said he, "I'm sorry you haven't had the courage to meet me lone. I can see now that I've lost before I begin. The judge is you, Dinah, and your mind is poisoned against me by cheap, bitter, sectional prejudices. And you have a corrupt jury as well. They're bought out before the trial begins."

"I dunno how much of that lingo we gotta stand!" burst out Bud Vincent.

"Leave him be! He's makin' his grandstand play, now," said Harry.

"Aye," said Alfred Clark. "I've tried to appeal to you people in every way I know. I've tried to convince you that I'm just, and reasonable, and fair-minded.

"I've been wrong. I came out here expecting to find the great, big-hearted, noble West—running a bit to flannel shirts, not very fond of razors or grammar but, nevertheless, honest, decent, faithful, brave, and true to what good men and women ought to be. And, instead, I've found miserable jealousy, cruelty, unfairness, and a general desire to bully and ruin a man too untrained to fight back, but who if he could meet you with your own weapons, would gladly fight you one by one until either he was shot down, or he had taught you all your lessons. Brutes that you are, like brutes you should be handled!"

He had started mildly, he thought. But his temper mastered him as he went on, until at the end he felt his indignation mount higher and higher.

They had been shocked by this outburst.

"Well," said Harry at last, "the plain fact is, we never wanted you from the first. You didn't belong. You didn't know cows. You didn't know ranchin'. What right had you on the place?"

"A contemptible conspiracy, I call it," said Alfred Clark. "This very moment you know that you're all prepared to work together and pull together in order to finish off the Libertad business which you've prevented me from completing. I brought you up here, in the hope that I could move you by making an appeal to the celebrated chivalry and decency of the Westerner. I wanted to point out to you that the work I have been trying to do is the work which was committed to my hands by the man whom you pretended to love so much. I wanted to ask you, almost on my knees, to help me try to execute his will. But I see that appeals are not in order. In your own hard eye, Dinah, I can read the message."

The girl stood up.

"Maybe you're partly right. Maybe we *haven't* given you the squarest break in the world. But certainly the best way now is for you to cut and go and let us try to wrangle our own affairs."

"Very well," said Clark. "I'm one man, and I can't stand against all of you—"

"Why not count *me* on your side, partner?" said a voice from a corner of the room.

By the second window, they could make out the form of a man who was leaning his shoulders against the wall, his hands in his trouser pockets. He must have entered through the window with silence worthy of a professional thief.

"Who are you?" asked Vincent, advancing a little.

"Why," said the stranger, "if it ain't little ol' Buddie Vincent, that regular man-killin', hoss-bustin' puncher! If it ain't ol' Buddie, the riot gun, and sharpshooter. Him that kills linnets on the wing at a hundred yards, and shoots the eyelashes off a wolf at half a mile. Why, doggone me, Buddie, how many men you murdered since I last seen you?"

He advanced into the light. It was Cayenne Charlie, his bruised and swollen face broadly smiling.

Bud Vincent moved forward, his hands fisted.

"Buddie!" snapped Dinah Clark.

And Vincent stepped suddenly back.

In spite of himself, Clark could not help admiring the manner in which the girl had controlled that wildcat.

"This is Cayenne Charlie," said Alfred Clark. "He's dropped in for a little talk."

"It's Red!" exclaimed Harry.

"I see you, old-timer," said Cayenne cheerfully. "I ain't met *you* yet, ma'am?" he said to the girl.

"This is Dinah Clark," said her uncle.

"And you're the fellow who smashed things up last night?" asked Dinah.

"No smashin'," said Cheyenne. "There was

just a little party up the street, and the police force of this here town got mixed in and warmed themselves up on me."

"How did you get free?" asked Harry.

"Easy. I pulled some bars off the door, grabbed a guard by the throat, made him unlock the cell, dropped him with a good punch on the button, took his gun, and here I am."

"He had an appointment with me here," Clark explained to the others, "at eight o'clock. And that's the hour now, as you see."

"Can I kinda give you a hand in the business you've got on deck here?"

"Frankly, that's exactly what I wanted to talk to you about," said Clark. "I didn't know how, but I hoped you might help me."

"Glad to try," said Cayenne. "Looks to me like this bunch has framed you."

Bud Vincent made a sound no louder than a whisper and reached inside his coat. Instantly, a bright revolver gleamed in the hand of Cayenne and covered the head of the youth.

"Right between the eyes is where you get it, son," said Cayenne, "if you so much as wink. And you back up, Harry, and carry your arms wide of your hips. I'm watchin' you both. Sorry, ma'am, to make all this trouble. But these here boys of yours, they're kind of restless."

He stepped to Vincent as he spoke, and dexterously removed two Colts from the person of the gunfighter.

"I'm going to have the heart out of you!" Vincent promised him.

"Sure you will," said Cayenne Charlie. "Set down and rest your feet, Buddie. Now you might try to recollect me, maybe. I'm the hobo that you hit with the chair up in Denver, just outside of town in that wayside tavern. But I don't carry a grudge. They got good jails in Colorado, and I enjoyed a mighty fine rest after the sheriff hauled me in."

He sat down on the edge of the table, and put away his gun. He had not disarmed big Harry, but instead, kept a watchful eye on him.

"Don't make a move, Harry," said the girl. "Charlie here is havin' himself a good time. Now, Cayenne, what's on your mind heavier than red hair?"

Alfred Clark was amazed by her good humor and easy way. She seemed not in the least affronted by the wildness of this battered jailbreaker.

"I'll tell you," said Charlie, "Me and my friend, here, are together. It sounds like you and the boys have been crowdin' him a little."

"D'you aim to help him play his hand?" she asked.

"No, I aim to get him a new deal."

"Where'll you find your cards?"

"Up my sleeve," said Cayenne.

"Go on," she said.

"The boss, here, is in town for cows. An' you an' the boys have stopped him." He turned to Alfred Clark. "Now, I know gents in this neck of the woods that'll give you a herd about any size you want, thirty per cent under market price, and delivered right on the border—for hard cash. Does that sound to you?"

"He's out of the picture, Cayenne," said the girl. "He's leaving for the East in another hour."

"Are you?" asked Cayenne. "Or are you stayin' with me?"

"My friend," said Alfred Clark, "I've been praying for some way of meeting these people on their own ground, with their own weapons, in order to make the ranch a go in spite of them. Cayenne, you dropped into this room out of heaven, so far as I'm concerned. Of course I'm staying."

"You promised me," began the girl. "And if you go back on the promise you—"

"I promised you that today I'd make up my

mind. Well, I've made it up. I stay!"

She was still cool, though a little pale.

"If you mean to sashay out to the ranch with this man for a big gun," she said, "you gotta remember that we have the place loaded down with fighting men. D'you think that he could handle the whole crowd—and with him a fugitive?"

"I think that he might be able to," said Alfred Clark.

"I'll tell you again, for the last time," she said. "The range is *my* place, and the only people who have a right to say a word about the running of it are the men that Daddy hired and who helped him to build it up. I can't see your claim to any position on it. I don't see why you want to be there."

"Because your father appointed me. You've arranged to have the ranch go downhill until I leave. Well, Dinah, now I think that I have a lever in my hand, and I intend to use it."

The girl made no retort to this last remark, but went through the door hastily, head high. Harry followed her without a word. Vincent would have done the same thing, but Charlie called him back.

"You've forgotten something, old son," said he.

Vincent wheeled and came slowly toward

the table, on which Cayenne had placed the weapons. He picked up the two Colts.

"I'll settle you, all in good time," said he, and he went out through the door.

Cayenne turned to Alfred Clark. "About the cows, chief, it'll take a week to get things together. A week from today, you show at Santa Cruz of the Willows on the river. The cows will come in there at night. They ought to be across the river before the next morning. Me, I've gotta barge along."

He went to the door, but after looking out, instantly stepped back.

"The law is out there. It's over the house-tops for me!"

He left Alfred Clark before the latter could speak a word. Like a bird, through the window, Cayenne Charlie had flown away.

They lay a half day's march north of the river. They had passed from Mexico into "God's country." The great mass of long-horned cattle, with their fierce eyes and scrawny bodies, had been bedded down for the night, and ahead of them rode three men on night watch.

After crossing the Rio Grande, at the long noon halt when the strength of the sun made traveling a doubtful virtue, Alfred Clark had gathered the men around him and he had made a speech.

"When I came out here, I had a duty to perform that looked to you like an intolerable imposition. You felt that you were able to run the ranch well enough and that any one among you—like Harry, for instance, would be able to manage affairs so that Dinah's interests would be well taken care of. As I saw it, I had a sacred duty to perform in executing the will of my dead brother. You felt that you were right. I felt that I was right.

"Now, through the assistance of Mr. Cayenne Charlie Bird, I've been put in the way of a stroke of business fortune which ought to more than recoup any losses that I have cost the ranch so far. You may say these cattle have been stolen, and that they're shady goods. Perhaps they are. I don't know. Everything, so far as I could see, was perfectly regular, except that the sellers wanted to have their cash upon the spot. Very well. I gave them their cash. Then my right to the cows—in Dinah's name—seemed well enough established. We have not lost hide nor hair of a single cow since the start.

"It is true that we have a distance to go still, through rough country, filled with rough men. Nevertheless, I feel almost as secure as though we were now at the home ranch. For

I believe that you men are going to work for me, realizing that I am not devoted to my own interests but to those of my niece, and I am convinced that all of you are devoted to her.

"As for me, I don't pretend to be an expert in cattle. I don't know anything about the management of a ranch, except such little odds and ends as I have been able to pick up since I came to this country. Nevertheless, I have asked for advice, and some of my mistakes I may put down to the fact that instead of giving me the best opinions, some of you have given me the worst.

"Well, I believe that we know each other better, now. If you'll stick by me and my niece, in one short year I'll be able to throw over the reins, she'll come to her majority, and then she can select her own manager.

"It may be unmanly to appeal to you, but I can't help begging you to stand by me. I beg you to help me fight this thing through."

When he had finished this novel speech, there were no directly spoken comments, but there were grunts and noddings of heads, here and there. Only Harry and Bud Vincent looked grimly down at the ground and said nothing. But Clark knew their secret rancor, and was not surprised.

On the whole, he felt that his appeal had

been successful, and certainly during the rest of that day the men had gone about their work with an apparent willingness.

He guessed, after the start, that the entire crowd had been amazed by his stroke of business, amazed that he was able to attach that furious and strange vagrant, Cayenne Charlie, to his fortunes, amazed that Cayenne had cared to live up to his contract by delivering the cattle as agreed beforehand.

As this evening settled in, Cayenne was gone, but he *had* kept his word. Clark went out to see how the herd was lying, and found it comfortably placed and apparently serene. Now and then there was a grunt and an upward lurch as some young animal was touched by the angrily swung horns of an older one.

The punchers on guard circled around and around, walking or jogging their horses, and singing low, endless, crooning songs which reassured the herd.

Clark could understand for the first time the fascination of the entire cattle business as he listened, and watched the dull gleam of starlight on the polished horns. What amazed him was that this vast mass of powerful life was submitting to the hands of so few men. There they lay, ready for the long journey to grasslands, markets, but leaving behind them young life which would grow in turn, and so would follow harvest after harvest, while God planted the grass and sent the rains which nourished it.

Peace descended upon the soul of Alfred Clark.

He took some coffee, ladling it out with a long dipper, sipping that bitter, hot brew. Munching soggy, sweet, corn pone, he squatted on his heels, puncher fashion, and felt that life was not so bad, though the collar of his coat scraped his sunburned neck. Other men had delighted in this life. He could delight in it himself. And, looking to the northwest, where the mountains rose in small waves against the stars, he felt as though he were already at the gate of success.

One of the night watch came in, dismounted, threw his reins, and poured a big tin cup full of coffee.

He was a raw-boned, sun-dried man named Chick Thomas. His hair was deep brown, and his long mustaches swept down and out.

This tall fellow possessed a certain style, Alfred Clark decided, with his slouchy, comfortable clothes, and the slight outward sagging of his legs, as if for strength and for the curve of a saddle. His trousers were tucked into his wrinkled boot-tops, a low-belted revolver dragged down from the right hip; there was a bandanna a little askew, the knot properly at the back of the neck; and upon his heels stood out the glistening lines of his spoon-handled spurs. Like the symbol of a belted knight, thought Alfred Clark.

Thomas stood at ease, drinking the coffee. In some mysterious manner, without putting down the big cup, he was able to roll a cigarette. As he lighted and puffed it, he spoke.

"Look at 'em," said Chick Thomas. "Quiet."

He gestured with the cup to indicate the herd, and Clark regarded them.

"They're very quiet," he agreed.

"Sure," said Chick. "I think they'll spend a good night."

Here a scream burst at them. It was distant, but so peculiarly shrill, and with such a pulse, that it seemed to run at them and swell closer and closer.

Then a chorus of wild shouts broke out on the northern verge of the herd. The whole mass of cows lurched to their feet. They spilled into groups and odd clusters, like iron filings over which a strong magnet had been rapidly passed.

"Stampede sure as fate!" said Chick Thomas without emotion, and leaped into the saddle of his horse.

From the camp wagon came the cook, literally flying, not speaking a word, but throwing a saddle on a hobbled horse with wonderful speed. The yells continued, and now they were broken and accompanied by a rapid rolling of pistol shots. With this, the entire herd swung about and bolted for safety— and safety in their eyes seemed to lie south, toward the Rio Grande.

Clark himself had hastily mounted.

He did not need to spur the horse. That strong-willed mustang flattened his ears and stretched out his neck to lower wind resistance, and began to run as though it were striving to blow the saddle off its back with the speed of its gallop.

Certainly, it very nearly blew off poor Alfred Clark. Never a good horseman, he dangled on one side of the animal and then on the other, with a sense that a starlit sea had risen upon the desert and was rushing at him with a vast and increasing roar.

But by keeping one hand strong on the pommel and the other strong on the mane of the horse, he managed to regain the saddle. Not six steps behind him was a low-headed wave of tossing, sharp horns, and glittering, fear-widened eyes, and a vast thunder was beaten out by the pounding of innumerable hoofs.

Fear jumped into the throat of Clark. He looked back and saw the cook wagon reel like a ship in a stormy sea. It toppled and disappeared.

After that, he looked straight ahead and rode for all he was worth, bending low. Certainly the mustang seemed to quicken beneath him in this new posture. They flew on. Looking to either side, he saw a long dark horn of stampeding animals stretching out before the rest. He actually felt that these arms were stretching for him, and that he was a doomed man!

With whip and spur he urged on the mustang, keeping a short hold on its reins, and so, by sweet degrees, he heard the snorting grow fainter behind him, while the roar of the hoofs diminished a little, and the bellowing no longer seemed directly in his ears.

He looked back, made sure that he was able to cross over the face of the herd to one flank, and pulled away to the side, across the wild front of this storm of animals.

What happened, he wondered? What had started the stampede?

Rustlers, perhaps!

He groaned, and heartily cursed the West

and all that it stood for in man and beast. The shining face of a varnished desk, that was the proper environment in which he should spend his days. Not this mountain desert—this place of torment.

He heard the beating of hoofs. Chick Thomas was beside him.

"What's happened, Thomas?"

"Dunno—but they're sure on the run."

A hundred steers burst from the flank of the herd and swept toward them. They rode for their lives.

His horse, Clark knew, might put its foot in a hole at any moment, and end his own life and that of his rider; but Clark kept on at a high gallop.

He could guess that, as the speed of the runners diminished, they would fan out and scatter. Even if the punchers wanted to do their best to save the herd it was probably true that half of the lot would be gone before morning. And, in that country, it would be very odd if they managed to recollect from the desert what malice or bad luck had spilled upon the face of it.

This was the end of his proud hopes. This was the last step. He would have to admit his failure.

Then he saw out of the thickest night before him, a rider who actually bolted straight in at the face of the fleeing ocean of cattle!

Moreover, behind this madman, who rode screeching like a wild Indian, came a string of four or five other riders who yelled as loudly as their leader.

Straight across the head of the running herd they swept, firing their guns.

The center of the herd began to slow. It whirled into a tangle.

The arms of free cattle upon either side continued to lurch forward, but these punchers, if such they were, swerved outward, and caught those horns at the tips, and bent in the flying streams. Never had Alfred Clark seen such wild riding, such utter abandon, such total recklessness.

The rear of the frightened herd came up with a rush and packed the mass, in the center, unbearably close and hard.

The thundering voice of the frightened, bewildered animals seemed to be rolling up from the solid earth at the feet of Clark's horse.

He could see little. The cloud of dust choked him to the bottom of his lungs. He kept passing a hand across his eyes, but only succeeded in rubbing the alkaline dust deeper into them, until he was more than half blinded.

He drew back his horse to a greater distance, so far that he was freed from the dust. Now he could see the picture as a whole, and it was a grand one, with the dust cloud mounting like smoke into the heavens, reaching, as it were, into the Milky Way; while from the earth where it rose, he could see the dim silhouettes of the whirled cattle.

There were side charges from the outer flanks of the herd, but every time, these charges were met by the adroit and fearless counterattacks of the punchers, who rode right in under the noses of the stampeding cows and fired off their guns.

So, finally, the stampede ended, and gradually the milling ceased. The herd settled. Some of them sank down from sheer exhaustion, stifled by the dust fumes. Others grew calm enough to follow that example. The dust cloud rose, cleared, becoming no more than a dim stain against the stars.

Who *were* these men who had stopped the herd? Why? For their own benefit? Did they intend that they should gather the cattle up, when they were sufficiently rested, and hurry them off in a new direction?

Then Clark had his answer.

Suddenly there was a loud, cheerful shout.

"Hullo, Clark! I been lookin' for you. That

was a grand game, eh?"

It was Cayenne Charlie!

They bedded the herd down where Charlie and his men had stopped the stampede. Of the six, three were Indian half-breeds, the outcross being Mexican blood. Two were pure-blooded Indians, gaunt as ravens and hardly more cheerful. One was a Negro with a weathered face.

Harry complained to Clark: "The boys won't work and ride with a sketchy lot like these fellows."

"Someone tried to stampede the herd," said Clark. "We don't know who it is, but they nearly succeeded tonight. With the help of Charlie's men we were able to beat off the attempt. We can't afford to throw such help away, can we?"

As he said this, he managed to keep his eyes openly and frankly upon the face of the other. He knew in his heart that Harry and his crowd certainly had connived, if they had not actually helped at the stampeding of the herd. And the ignorant malice of these men amazed him. He had been of a mind, before this, to believe that mere pique at the tenderfoot and presuming outlander had made them act such a bad part; but now he began to think that the men themselves were thoroughly a bad lot, perhaps well kept in hand by the great force of his brother, but now ready to run riot. His determination to stay with the work became fixed. He could not allow the place to be trusted to such a wild crew.

Harry went off, muttering, and Clark sought out Charlie.

"Tell me straight," he said to Cayenne. "Do you think *my* crew started the stampede?"

"I sure wouldn't say they done it direct," declared Charlie. "But it's kinda likely that they passed the word to a gang of rustlers that it was okay to come in and take the herd. Meaning your punchers would be all sort of out of the way when the stampede began. That's how I see it."

"Cayenne, I'd like to know what made you follow us with your men?"

"Suppose," said Charlie, "that you seen a sheep dog startin' out to run wolves, wouldn't you wanta foller along and keep an eye on him?"

"These men you've brought—are they trustworthy?"

"Yeah, so long as you've got a gun over 'em and the fear of the bullet in 'em. No, this crowd of mine ain't much good. But they work cheap, and they fight cheap, and if any of 'em get plugged in the fightin', it's only a quicker trip to the end that they're already overdue at. Your crew might or might not be a bad lot. But I *know* that mine are no good at all."

And they laughed together.

Cayenne Charlie continued his rounds at a walking pace, or sometimes jogging his horse softly. And sometimes, too, he would sing.

He was happy. It was rare for him to have so many good times crowded together. There had been the good, soul-filling saloon fight in Libertad to begin with; then the jail break; the pleasure of rounding up the six thugs, and finally the battle with the herd upon this night.

And as he journeyed on around the edges of the big herd, he had a joyous feeling that more trouble lay ahead of him, and the fore-taste was like the bouquet of old wine.

So the darkness deepened. Then he noticed that the stars in the east were growing dim, the mountains more black—and at last the soft gray of the dawn commenced.

Seven of the entire herd had been trampled to death, or died of fright and exhaustion. The rest were apparently unharmed, though a little wilder. And, in this order, without the loss of a single additional head, they made the long march through the rising hills beyond the desert to the Clark ranch.

They came through the southern pass into the big amphitheater which composed the ranch. Its treasure was water, which ran in four streams, not overlarge, down the sides of the valley and joined in the center of the Clark River.

Coming to meet them, Dinah broke through the windy mist and came in riding a beautiful, slender, bay gelding, a fiery four-year-old with the grace of a wildcat and much the same disposition.

"You've done it, Uncle Alfred!" she cried. "I've been sitting up here shaking my head, all this time, but here you are. I take off my hat to you. I've been a silly, sulky fool."

There was no hidden meaning, no secret smile. She looked at him with radiant eyes and his hand still tingled from the grasp of hers. He could see that as far as she was concerned, this one success had banished the past. There was something in her manner that, for the thousandth time, reminded him so sharply of his brother that his heart ached. But it was a pleasant sorrow, this time.

"The herd was brought together by Cayenne Charlie. It was on a ruinous stampede when Charlie and his men came up and put an end to it."

"And who brought Charlie inside the fold?" she asked. "You did, Uncle Alf, and, therefore, you get the credit. Hullo, Harry. This looks like the best bunch we ever got up from Old Mexico, eh?"

"It's a good bunch," said Harry.

"How you boys gettin' along with Charlie?"

"Good enough to please you, Dinah, I hope."

His horse lurched away, and the girl looked after him with a pucker of her brows.

"He's sore all the way through," she decided. "But let him get over it. He's all right, but he ain't the only man in the world. Hullo, Cayenne! Glad to see you. What's the news?"

"The news is that cows'll raise the dust, and the wind'll sure blow it. You look like you been eatin' three squares a day. Where'd ya get that wildcat anyway?"

He jerked his hand toward the horse, and Uncle Alfred looked on bewildered. With such ease and speed did the young men and women of today glide from subject to subject.

"This is a prime good one," said the girl.

"Yeah. Good to bust your neck," said he. "He's a sidewindin' fool, ain't he?"

"How'd ya know that?"

"I knew a first cousin of his once. He busted three ribs for me, gettin' introduced."

"Yeah?" said the girl. "But this one here is silk, what I mean to say."

"Slippery like silk, maybe. You better watch that baby, Dinah. He's gunna pile you, one of these days."

"Oh, he ain't so bad. You just gotta watch his ears a little. Try him. He steps out like a dancer."

"These here rocks look pretty hard," Charlie said. "I'd rather try him in the spring, when things is softer."

"Lookit him!" said the girl to Alfred Clark, laughing. "Trying to pretend to be afraid!"

"It ain't pretending," said Charlie. "They's too much white in his eyes to please me. But slide off and I'll take a chance."

She dropped to the ground and handed him the reins, holding his own roan mustang by the bridle. A Roman-nosed brute was this, with the build of an Indian pony—mostly stomach, and very little legs to him.

The girl regarded this brute for a moment, then prepared to mount.

The gelding, in the meantime, was spinning in a circle to embarrass his would-be rider, but Cayenne Charlie found his time and was into the saddle with a bound. His feet fell into the stirrups instantly, and the next moment the bay was trying to bump a hole in the blue of the sky. Cayenne sat him with amazing ease until he saw the girl swinging into his own saddle.

"Hey, get down from there!" he yelled. "That ain't a lady's hoss! That's nitroglycerine with a tight cork in the bottle. He'll blow up and bust!"

The roan, obediently as it were, immediately exploded. There was no other word for it. He seemed to disappear in an unjointed, spinning mist of striking and kicking legs. He whirled, he leaped, he sunfished. He began to spin like a top. And the girl shot from the saddle.

Alfred Clark cried out in an agony of fear as she pitched the hard ground, rolled over and over, and then lay still. But Cayenne Charlie reached the spot before him.

"You gone and busted something?" said Charlie, his face stern and white.

"No," said she. "I just got a mite dented, I guess. He's got a punch in him, that little old Solomon-nosed runt of a roan of yours."

"Stand up!" said Cayenne fiercely.

"Gimme a chance for my head to clear. I never seen the earth go around so fast before."

"Stand up!" repeated Cayenne. He took her

beneath the armpits and jerked her roughly to her feet. She reeled, reaching for support. "I'm all right!" she gasped.

"You ain't broke a leg or a hip," he decided critically. "How's your arms?"

"I dunno. Not much feeling in 'em just now."

Her clothes were torn, and she was covered with dust. Her mouth was black with it.

"I guess maybe he didn't crack you," said Cayenne. "The next time I tell you something, you do what I tell you. You hear me talk? You oughta be turned over somebody's knee and spanked. That's what I mean. A doggone nuisance is what you are!"

She nodded. "That *was* a fool play. I might've known that horse of yours was pure dynamite. I'm going to be black-and-blue for a week."

"Serve you right," said Cayenne Charlie. "One of these days, you're gunna go sashaying out on a high-steppin' hoss, and when you come back, it's gunna be on a door. You're gunna get piled, and you're gunna get busted, is what I mean!"

"I don't suppose you've been piled very often, Charlie."

"I been piled on every inch of my head," he answered deliberately. "I've been slammed on my shoulders, on my back. I've broken both legs three times. I've been dropped every place, and the worst place is flat on your face, believe me. It sort of makes you sit up and think."

And then Charlie Bird muttered: "I've gone and got all heated up. I've made a fool of myself."

"No, you haven't at all," she told him earnestly.

At this, he lifted his head and turned his still battered and discolored face toward her.

"I'll tell you how it was," he confessed. "When I seen that brute spinning, and seen you leaning out in the saddle, all I could look at was the rocks. I said to myself that you was a goner—" He stopped short, and took a great breath. "Well, thank Heaven!" said Cayenne Charlie.

Dinah said nothing. She looked straight before her, but it was plain that she was moved.

"I'll say one thing for you," said Charlie at last, "you're dead game. I never saw gamer!"

He paused, eyes narrowed.

"I had a sister," said Charlie, "who loved horses—as you love them. She'd had falls, but still she seemed to believe that the ground would always receive her softly. And she liked to see a hot thoroughbred come out of the stable door on his hind legs, walking like a bear with a couple of grooms dangling in the air from his bridle reins. That was what she considered a good beginning for a day's riding. Then, one day, the horse came home without her."

Here he fell silent, and tilted his head back, as a man will do who finds it a trifle hard to breathe freely.

"Was she young?" asked Dinah gently.

"She was fifteen," said Cayenne Charlie. He paused again, his face dark. "We loved her," said he, "beyond words to tell of it."

Alfred Clark looked at the girl. He could see, at a glance, that her lips trembled, and that her gaze was fixed straight before her, and that there was a brimming moisture in her eyes.

They reached the old camp in the early evening. Harry wanted the cattle to be scattered at once so that they might graze, whereas Cayenne Charlie insisted that they ought to be kept bunched and under guard.

Harry faced Alfred Clark. "All I wanta know," he said, "Is Cayenne the foreman, now?"

"He's not the foreman," replied Clark.

"Then will you say what we're to do with

the cows? They're dead beat. They been on the trail for a long time, and they oughta have a quick chance at this grass. We're gunna have a storm up this way, too, and it's likely to hit us tonight. You can see the way the clouds are bankin' up high on the north mountains, there. They're likely to let out wind, and thunder, and lightnin', and it's better for the cattle to have a chance to scatter around and get shelter."

This seemed reasonable enough. Clark looked at Cayenne, and found that Charlie was scowling.

"Whacha up to, Harry?" said he. "What's the game, I'd like to know?"

"Let's hear your side of the case, Cayenne?" asked Clark.

"My side," said he, "is that these here cows need a good rest, and they ain't gunna get it if they're wanderin' around in batches. A cow is a lonesome critter and likes its own home pasture, and if you turn 'em loose without no guard to ride 'em close, they're gunna have a miserable time of it. By the mornin', you'll find 'em scattered over every part of the valley, and you can take my word for it!"

At this, Harry turned on his heel and marched off, without waiting for the official answer of Alfred Clark.

"He's soaked full of poison," said Cayenne Charlie.

"I think we'd better humor him," said Clark. "At least for now."

"Whatever you say."

"Charlie, there's another thing that I want to talk to you about."

"Fire away."

"It's not an easy thing to talk about, but perhaps I'm old enough to do it safely. You've dropped into Dinah's life like a hawk out of a blue sky. She's never known anybody like you. You're a hero, in her eyes, and loaded with romance. She's a wild, impressionable young girl."

Cayenne Charlie grew dark. "I'm tryin' to foller you, old son," said he. "Just go soft and slow."

"I believe you're a gentleman. I think I can trust you. I want you to look at Dinah, look at yourself, consider the future—and then act accordingly."

With that, he left Charlie and went to seek out Dinah.

They talked about Charlie, and about the crew's hatred of him.

"Why should they hate him?" asked Dinah.

"He's made them into a herd of fools. And

worse than that, he's treated you like a four-year-old child—and you've shown that you liked the treatment."

She flushed hotly.

"Well, are they wrong? Wasn't it plain to them as it is to me that Charlie has turned your head?"

"Rot," said she.

"Is that an honest answer?" he demanded.

"No," said she. "I'm pretty dizzy, all right. I never met such a fellow."

"Well," said Clark, "the more the old hands see you smiling at Charlie, the sicker they are going to become of their work, the valley, and you. They're apt to leave."

"Did they expect me to marry one of them?" she asked.

"Would that have shocked you so much, a week or so ago?"

"What are you driving at?"

"Suppose that Bud Vincent, with his easy ways and his handsome face, had asked you for the tenth time to marry him and—"

"Did he dare to tell you that he'd asked me before?" cried the girl.

"I'm a very dull-eyed old uncle, Dinah, but I didn't have to be told what a blind man could have guessed. You weren't really horrified at the idea of marrying one of those bold,

223

dashing fellows, and making him the king of this round table, with all the other punchers about you as paladins around the big chief? It seemed a pretty romantic life to you, didn't it? Something to look forward to?"

"Well, perhaps it did."

She confessed it suddenly. "You make me feel that I've been a fool, Uncle Alfred!"

"No, but you've been pretty young, and you're not much older, today. Mind you, I'm not advising. I'm not criticizing. I'm simply pointing out what appears to me a good political attitude for you to take."

"Tell me one thing."

"Whatever I can."

"Has Charlie said anything to you?"

"Not a word."

"Did you say anything to him?"

"Yes, I did."

"Good heavens! What?"

"Nothing to hurt his feelings, or yours. But something that may make him do a little thinking. Which I hope you'll find time for, also!"

And he left her.

It was a wild night. The wind rose and flowed against the house like a river in spate.

Cowpunchers might sleep on a night like

this, but not Alfred Clark. He lay for a long time awake, telling himself that there was nothing to be nervous about, though the place quivered and shook violently. But after a time there was a dizzy heeling of the house.

This got him out of bed in a hurry and he ran shivering to the window.

What he saw amazed him.

He had been conscious of a steady, loud, and angry roaring which he had taken, naturally for the voice of the wind, but now he saw that the Clark River was flooding its banks! There had been gusts of rain, like musketry, to be sure, but certainly not a sufficient downpour to account for this rising of the flood. He rolled his eyes, bewildered, to seek for a cause.

There was ample moonlight to enable him to see the entire valley on this side of the river. For though the south wind brought throngs of clouds across the sky, they were not sheeted solidly from horizon to horizon. Instead, they went in fleets and in single masses, cruising with an incredible speed. They swept so close above the house that he could see the hulls of these torn and ragged craft, and then at a little distance they rushed on with the moon making their upper sections as translucent as sails.

These argosies of moisture sailed full tilt

to the northeast and there gathered, and wrecked in dense masses upon the slopes of Mount Fortune.

He could see the lofty, glistening head of the mountain, but its great shoulders and all its body were lost under cloaks of darkness, for there the clouds piled in ranks.

Now and then lightning jerked through the masses from head to plain and showed the long tresses of the descending rain that touched the foot of the mountain.

That was the source of the Clark River's rise. Yonder on those great slopes the rain must be bucketing down and it was no wonder that the river ran as white as milk and brimmed its banks.

He heard a booming report, wind-muffled. Again and again it was repeated.

Then he saw the cause.

The big swinging door at the near end of the largest barn had blown free from its fastenings.

He answered a light, quick knock at his door. He opened it to Dinah.

"There's something wrong, Uncle Alf," said she.

"The wind, you mean?" he asked her.

"That door of the barn, slamming. If there were any men in the bunkhouse, they certainly would be up and closing it."

"If there were any men in the bunk-house—" he repeated. "But, of course, it's full of men, Dinah!"

"Well, then," said she, "they're tied hand and foot, or else they'd go out and fix that door."

"I'll go and see," he said.

"I'll go with you."

He huddled into some clothes, and hastily went down stairs, buckling a revolver about him and hoping that he would not need it.

He found the girl waiting for him just outside the door of the house in a broad sweep of moonlight, for no cloud shadows were passing at that moment.

The wind had fallen a good deal, and still was dropping, though it was strong enough in separate gusts.

They went straight out to the bunkhouse, Clark carrying a lantern, and when they showed the light of it through the open door, it gave back a scene of the confusion: the clothes which had hung on the walls had been thrown down, chests and bags had been opened, and part of the contents scattered here and there.

"They've packed up their best belongings and got out," said Dinah. "Let's see what's left in the horse corrals."

She hurried straight off toward the corrals, and there they saw a number of animals lying down, close to the shelter of the barn, while a few stood disconsolately, facing the wind, miserable, glistening with rain.

"I don't see Chick's mustang," she said. "And that dark-pointed chestnut that Cleve Daniels always liked. He's gone, too; and the little black mare is gone—they've cleaned out, Uncle Alf. They've cleaned out and stolen horses to get away on!"

"But Charlie—somehow, I can't imagine that he would be beaten—" Clark muttered.

"What chance?" cried the girl passionately. "What chance would even Charlie have against a gang of cruel, selfish killers? That's what they are! I can see it now. Daddy could handle them—but he was the only man who could."

They returned to the bunkhouse, went in.

The floor was littered. Beds had been ripped up, perhaps because some of the treasures of the punchers had been sewed into the sacking, and the straw was scattered, lifting and rustling in the draft. Old magazines lay about, fluttering their yellowed pages. Boots with rumpled tops; shoes whose soles had been worn through; battered hats; dunnage bags sometimes only half emptied; tattered shirts, underwear—all the garb of cowpunchers lay heaped and tangled about them.

Alfred Clark, with an odd feeling of one walking a deserted battlefield, moved slowly here and there until, with a start, he saw the body of a man lying face downward on a bunk in the corner of the room.

He pulled out his revolver and raised the lantern. Beyond doubt, it was a man, and even at the distance, he could see the great, ghastly red wound that gaped across the top of his head.

"It's Charlie!" Dinah cried. "I knew it! I knew it!" She ran to the bunk.

Clark followed her, dizzy with horror. The memory of the man in all his strength and courage filled his mind.

When he came to the bunk, she had turned Charlie Bird on his side, and her face was pressed close to his heart.

Presently one of her hands began to lift and fall with a slow, irregular, faltering rhythm, and suddenly he understood. She was counting pulsations of the heart; Charlie Bird still kept some feeble remnant of life in him.

She got to her knees. Dauntlessly she examined the wound in the head. "A scalp wound. That's all. And the curs thought they'd killed him!"

They cleansed the wound. They closed the gaping lips of the cut and poured a stiff dram of brandy down Cayenne's throat. Charlie sat up, gave one wandering glance to the confusion of the room about him, then started to his feet.

That move was too sudden even for his uncanny strength, and he staggered, until Alfred Clark caught him by the shoulder.

The man was iron. Half-stunned as he still was, the shoulder muscles writhed and played like steel coils under the grasp of Clark.

Charlie rubbed a hand across his forehead.

"D'you know who it was, Charlie?" asked Clark. "Who struck you down?"

"I dunno. They told me that Buddie Vincent wanted to see me outside. I thought that Bud had changed his mind and wanted to fight it out so I went to see him. And as I stepped through the door, somebody dropped me from behind. So . . . . they've cleared out, have they?"

"Yes."

"By their whisperin' together all evenin' long, I guessed that that was what they were up to. My boys—are they gone, too?"

"Yes," nodded Clark. "There are only the three of us left on the place."

"Which way did they make their drive?"

"Drive?" asked Clark.

"If they're gone, they've taken the cattle with them! Don't you see? As long as they thought that they had the ranch in their hands, they were willing to let things go along peacefully. But when they saw that there was to be a change and the ranch was not for them, then they made up their minds pretty quick."

He was keen, alert; suffering almost no reaction from the blow which had stunned him so completely.

"How long ago did this happen?" asked the girl.

"About half past ten. What time is it now?"

"Nearly one."

He groaned, snapping his fingers with impatience. "That gives them a long start. We'll have to move."

They followed him outside.

On Mount Fortune the thickness of the rain mist was abating, but the Clark River seemed to be running higher than ever.

"Now tell me quick," said Cayenne Charlie. "Where's their market?"

"Straight down through the north pass," said the girl.

"How far is it?"

"Twenty miles."

"Then that's where they runnin' the herd."

"How could they get cattle across the river?" asked Dinah.

"It wasn't so high, earlier. They could have made the drive at that time. But it'll be the devil's own work gettin' across now."

"What can the three of us do against the lot of them?" asked Alfred Clark.

"We need to ride, not talk!" snapped Charlie.

And they saddled three of the fastest horses.

At the river, they found the bank worn and cut by the sharp hoofs of hundreds of the cattle which had been thrust down this shoot into the stream.

Charlie Bird rode in until his horse was knee-deep, but it was instantly apparent, from the way the current boiled around the legs of the horse, that they could not cross here.

"Higher up?" he shouted, above the roar of the river. "Is there a better crossing higher up the stream?"

"It's like this clear to the foot of Mount Fortune," answered Dinah. "It's no good, Charlie. There's no way of getting across."

He turned his head and stared again at the

stream. A tree went by. It must have been torn from a bank on the mountain itself, for no trees grew on the plain. It struck a riffle, and shot half its length high into the air, then dropped from sight in the swirling mass.

That stream was traveling like the wind. Its force was incalculable. Yet Cayenne Charlie rode down the verge. He took the rope which was coiled at the bow of Clark's saddle and carefully fastened an end of it to his own lariat.

They came to a point where the current narrowed. The water shot by as dark and smooth as steel, and just around the bend roared a cataract. They could see the leaping spray of it dancing like pale jewels in the light of the moon.

"I'm going across," said Cayenne Charlie suddenly.

"You *can't!*" cried Dinah. "There's no way—"

"There's always a way if a man can find it," he said, and turning the horse from the river he took it doubling back at frantic speed. On the verge of the bank he spurred deep, and the tormented animal leaped wildly forward.

They saw the rider strike the water, disappear, and then as he came to the surface cast the noose of his rope toward one of the rocks that fringed the northern shore.

The cast failed, and instantly, despite the struggling of the horse, the river whirled Cayenne Charlie toward the rapids. Dinah was riding her own horse into the water, crying out.

The rope had been gathered rapidly back into the hands of Cayenne, and now, even while the horse was spinning with him, out shot the noose again. It soared . . .

And fell fair and true over the head of a big rock.

The next moment the line was taut. It vibrated out of sight in the moonlight; it was holding, and by hauling mightily on it, Charlie was drawing himself and the horse in toward the farther shore.

They reached the shallows and clambered out onto the safety of firm land.

The crossing was simple now.

A rock tied to the end of the line enabled Charlie to throw it across. It was made fast at either end and Dinah was instantly in the water.

Once, it seemed she would be pulled from the saddle by the grip on the rope and the pull of the stream against the horse. But they worked through, and Alfred Clark followed after them.

It was, as a matter of fact, less terrible than

he had imagined, as he came safely across to the farther slope.

There he found Cayenne Charlie laughing, his teeth glittering in the moonlight.

"We're winning! We're winning!" he said. "We couldn't have such a good start without a good ending. Now which way for the pass, and let's ride like the wind!"

Like the wind they rode, in fact. The ground leaped away behind them in great pulsations as the horses galloped on. They spared horseflesh not a whit on this night, but made fine speed across the level, and then through the hills which rose first gently, and then with steeper sides as they got in toward the northern pass. And always the girl rode in front, showing the way.

When a very steep pitch slowed the horses to a walk, and bunched them closely together, she said: "If the herd is still in the pass, we can get up there to the side and from the gap between those two hilltops we can start a brush fire. They could see that down in Las Atlas. That's the signal we've arranged. When they see that, the sheriff will come humming!"

As their horses strained over the top of the rise, they saw beneath them the dark throat of the pass, filled, lined, and glittering with the moon-brightened horns of thousands of cattle.

Cayenne Charlie did not hesitate. He sent his horse down the slope like a falling stone, and Clark, with a groan of fear, nerved himself and started to gallop after. He found Dinah at his side, screaming wildly at him: "Let him go! We can't help Charlie in the fight. We can only help by getting the fire going up there in the gap!"

He saw her point instantly.

The signal, once sent, might bring help in time. But if all three of them were swallowed up in the gorge, then the punchers could surround them and take them at their ease. So Clark swerved his horse to the side and rode with the girl straight back for the gap between the hills.

They could hear the noise of guns behind them. No doubt the punchers had seen the wild man coming and opening fire.

Clark twisted in the saddle, looking back. Yes, plainly he could see the leader who rode at the head of the herd dismount, take his reins over one arm, kneel, and level his rifle.

It was Bud Vincent, intent on killing the man he hated most. Once and again that rifle spoke, as Charlie rushed in. His own revolver leaped in the moonlight and answered.

A single shot.

Vincent stood up, threw aside his rifle as if in triumph—but both hands were pressed against the spreading crimson at his chest. He toppled forward, with Cayenne Charlie's bullet in his heart.

Now Clark and the girl were at the top of the rise. Before them, they could see the distant lights of Las Altas down the grade. And behind, and to the side, but infinitely closer, was the herd jammed in the throat of the pass, frightened, milling, beginning to bellow like thunder through which the cracking of the guns continued. They could still see Cayenne Charlie. He had ensconced himself in a nest of rocks in the very heart of the pass.

Clark set frantically to work in the brush, collecting dry wood for the fire which must be built at once. Could it be done?

Dinah had a small ax with which she was busy. For his own part, he was tearing frantically at the brush with his bleeding, naked hands.

He got a heap of tinder together, unwrapped his matches from their oiled silk. He groaned and struck a match.

It went out. So did another and another. But at last he had a glimmer of flame! He put his match to the piled brush. Dinah had another match lit which she also applied. The brush ignited slowly, a red core, like a fierce eye. It gained, it grew. It spread. The match singed his fingers and dropped, but still the new flame continued.

With trembling hands, they fed it with twigs, fanned it. Clark knelt over it as over an altar.

The whole of the flames were choked in thick white smoke. Then right up above the smoke appeared a glimmering red hand. The whole bush took fire with a rush and a roar!

"Stay here! Keep the fire going!" cried Alfred Clark. "I must help Cayenne!"

"Wait!" she protested. "You're no gun-fighter. They'll kill you!"

Clark looked into the valley. Indeed, it seemed a pit of death to him. He could see the guns of the punchers flickering in the moon-light, and where the shadow lay, the flash of the explosions. They were forming a circle around the rocks in which Cayenne Char-lie lay, fighting back with a shot now and again.

"I'm going down there!" cried Alfred Clark. "If I've lived like a worm all my life, I'm going to die like a man, at least!"

He heard the tingling cry of her protest be-hind him. But he spurred his horse frantically forward. He felt the hissing cold of the wind in his teeth as he went down that steep descent.

Then a man stood up from behind a rock, shooting at him with a rifle, calmly, deliberately.

It was Harry.

Alfred Clark snatched out his revolver and fired blindly in return.

The rifleman disappeared! Had Harry been hit? No matter, the danger was past.

Clark was now in the heart of the pass. He skirted hundreds of frightened cattle. They were running aimlessly, or turning in great confused wheels, and the reechoed, redoubled thunder of their bellowing stunned his ears. It was as though he were already dead, and riding through the uproar of an inferno.

Wasps hummed past his face. Bullets? Yes, of course.

There was the gleaming little nest of rocks before him.

"Welcome, ole son!" cried Cayenne Charlie.

Clark flung himself from his horse, while that good animal, with tossing reins, fled on up the pass. Then Clark was kneeling, shuddering inside the mock circle, and Charlie was laughing, and roughly clapping him on the back.

"This'll break their hearts for 'em!" Charlie declared. "They've got *two* mysteries to deal with now. A dead man come back at them, and you on the warpath, at last. Keep close to the rocks. How much ammunition have you? Twenty rounds? Better than twenty million dollars to me, just now! Ah, that was a grand thing, that charge down the slope. I didn't know you could ride like that. Well, with the sheriff on his way we've *got* 'em!"

The firing had ceased suddenly after the arrival of Clark at the little natural fort. And then Clark, with a leap of his heart, saw a man skulking close to their rocks.

The rifle of Cayenne Charlie was instantly up. The other rose suddenly: "Don't shoot!" he called. "I'm with you, boys!"

He came running forward toward them. He leaped over the rim of the rocks, and dropped down again, a rifle in either hand. It was big Chick Thomas.

A wild, piercing yell of rage broke out from those who had watched.

"I never liked the dirty business," said Thomas. "I never liked it, and when I saw you come chargin' down, Clark, I swore that I'd be a man, too. Thank Heaven they didn't finish you, Cayenne. That was the stroke that turned me sick of 'em!"

"They're licked, and they know it," said Clark.

"Aye," agreed Cayenne. "They'll never bust the herd through this pass. Not now. Not with three rifles to stop 'em."

He was right. It was the beginning of a new era for the Clark ranch. A new era for Alfred Clark, also.

Dinah built him a house exactly to his taste in a pleasant corner of meadow grass beside a creek, with a hill and a grove to cheer him. There he installed his books. There he brought his Boston terrier. There he settled quietly into a serene life. He could not leave. She would not let him.

"You've proved that Daddy was right, putting his trust in you," Dinah told him. She turned to grasp the hand of her new husband. "And you've been more than a good ranch manager, Uncle Alfred, you've been a prospector—and you've found me a man!"

And she smiled up into the eyes of Cayenne Charlie Bird.

The Golden Day

Composed in Italy at Faust's hillside villa overlooking the Renaissance towers of Florence, this short story was completed in late May of 1930, as Faust turned 38.

In "The Golden Day" (printed the following year in *Liberty*), Faust was fictionally revisiting his youth in California, when he worked long, back-breaking hours as a farm and ranch hand in order to survive. The daily chores of his protagonist, Jim Eagan, had all been Faust's as a young man—and the fierce barroom brawl forming the story's climax echoed dozens of bruising fist fights he had experienced in those early days.

No stampedes or blazing six-guns here, just the raw reality of a hardworking man of the soil who battles for love and honor.

A simple, superbly crafted tale of the "new" West.

For thirteen days at a stretch Jim Eagan rose at five and worked until dark; even after supper he often patched harness or sharpened plowshares in the blacksmith shop until his bedtime, for the land of his hill farm was poor, and although he multiplied his hands and his hours in this fashion he got on very slowly; often the loans on his crops nearly equaled their value. On alternate Sundays he drove his Ford thirty miles through the uplands down to Tucker Flat and Tuckerville to see Kate Martin.

This morning in mid-March was only Thursday of the week. He had cut from the shelf of the stack hay for the cows in the corral; he had fed, curried, and harnessed the mules in the barn; he had loaded the light wagon with redwood posts for the fence which he was building to separate the southeast forty acres of summer fallow from the hillside pasture; and still the sun was not up when he started for the house with the first bucket of milk. The sun was not up, but something on the hills made Eagan turn about and stare at them, the heavy bucket swinging slowly at the end of his arm.

All the slopes were glowing. The poppies were out. They must have been blooming for days and days, but labor had stooped the head of Eagan so that when he walked out he saw little but the ground before him and the square toes of his boots stepping on it. He stood there so long that his shoulder began to ache. He drew in a deep breath, then went on to the house.

He finished the milking, strained the milk into the shallow tin setting pans, put them on the shelves, and went in to cook his breakfast. The barn, where the mules were stamping and grinding at their hay, seemed a cheerful place compared with the stillness and the damp shadow which filled his house.

When he kindled the fire it strangled for a moment in its own fumes, but the draft took hold presently and the flames jumped up the chimney with a roar.

He poured three cups of cold water over three heaping tablespoonfuls of coffee and put the pot over the strongest part of the fire. He cut from a remnant of a side of bacon, home-cured, four good thick slices. As it began to fry, into the grease he sliced two potatoes, boiled the evening before. He left the skins on; he had an idea that the good of the potato was in or near the skin. Then he slid a pan filled with fragments of corn bread into the oven, and in twenty minutes his meal was ready to take from the stove. He sat down with his heels hooked around the table legs and consumed the food.

Nearly every breakfast was the same. Eagan kept chickens, but the eggs brought such a good price that he would not waste them on himself. Whether he ate little or much seemed to make small difference. His strength of body and of nerve was a reservoir never drained, and winter or summer his weight varied not two pounds.

The sun was up and the day was well begun as he finished his third cup of coffee, the smallest, bitterest, blackest cup of the three. He rolled a cigarette out of brown wheat-straw papers and sweet pipe tobacco. It burned crookedly and soon the smoke became scalding hot, but the mouth of Jim Eagan was lined with iron. He inhaled to the bottom of his lungs and blew out slowly through his nose and mouth until there was a blue-brown cloud between him and the window, and beyond the window poured the brilliance of the outer day.

The fire had died down. The room was already chill again, and out of the dank shadow and through the mist of his own making he looked at the brilliance of the morning. Jim Eagan shuddered a little as he did on a gray winter day when he followed the plow, walking through grass which was crystal white with frost; this day the winter was in his heart.

"I'll get out," said Eagan to the cloud of tobacco smoke. "I'll go to town."

So he washed the dishes, swept the floor, made the bed, and went out to the barn. When he opened the door of it, the sight of the harnessed mules and the way they turned their heads to him roused up his guilty conscience. He took the harness off them slowly, badly hurt by remorse and self-contempt, but when he turned out the mules and saw them run on to the green of the pasture, shaking their heads and switching their tails, incredulous and joyful, some of his melancholy left him, and his sense of guilt.

It would do them good, that extra day off. Yellow, white, and blue gleamed on the close-cropped grass of the pasture. Over the naked bones of the elm trees beyond, a silver smoke of land mist was rising, but even through the mist he could see the flame of the poppies that rippled up the hillside.

With big strides he went back to the house.

In his bedroom he stripped off his clothes. Then he went out on the back porch, poured a bucket of cold water into a laundry tub of galvanized iron, and scrubbed himself with yellow laundry soap and a stiff brush. A breeze came out of the west and laid icy fingers on him, puckering his skin and turning it bluish white about the knees, but he looked down at the lean, hard strength of his body and smiled at the wind.

Standing at the verge of the porch, he flung out the dirty water, poured in a fresh bucket and rinsed thoroughly with it; then he dried himself and went back to his bedroom. There he dressed in a suit of blue serge, well pressed and spotless, and pulled on a pair of high shoes for which he had paid eight dollars several years before. He flexed his toes and admired the flawless suppleness of the leather. It paid to get the best now and then. Once a week he polished those shoes; twice a month he wore them.

He was always a man to face the facts, and therefore he faced himself in the mirror. Eagan was twenty-nine, but he admitted that he looked years older. The coat which once had fitted so perfectly now was a trifle snug across the back and a trifle loose across the breast. He had begun to stoop. Even the good iron of which he was made was yielding a little.

But what the farm made of him he must accept. He had invested in it the faith of ten years of labor and therefore the land was sacred. He completed the picture of himself which Tuckerville and Kate should see with a silk handkerchief carefully tucked into the breast pocket of his coat so that the corner of it projected. Then, into a towel, he rolled a clothesbrush, hairbrush, comb, and small mirror; he put on a pair of chamois gloves and went out to the Ford.

It was an open delivery-wagon model which he had bought secondhand. Of all the running parts and the engine he took his usual perfect care, but lack of paint and loose mud guards flapping and rattling did not disturb Jim Eagan. At the first whirl of the starting crank the motor roared, and in another moment he was on the road to Tuckerville.

He drove very slowly as far as his land extended. His plowed ground, over the level and up the slopes, made an irregular pattern; again and again it invaded the rocks, but they were as aggressive as he, putting out stern peninsulas and headlands into the heart of his richest meadows. Two forbidding islands arose in the forty acres of summer fallow and other islands stood here and there like shapeless boats at anchor in the sea of green. Year by year the margins of those islands grew as the rocks thrust their heads above the surface of the fields and had to be pried up and carried away.

He used to say that he had the best ground

in the world, for it could produce a ton of hay and a ton of rocks to the acre, but there was always sorrow in his heart and dread of the future when he made the jest. Hope was no dazzling light in the soul of Eagan; for ten years he had fought like a soldier until he had cleared away the last defiling trace of a mortgage and now he looked forward only to some minor degree of comfort, and Kate Martin.

Above the rattling of the car the songs of the meadowlarks flashed against his ear and were gone. The smell of damp soil and of growth was in the air.

When the car slid out from the hills; he found Tucker Flat on fire with spring blossoms from Loren's Gulch to the town. In the meadows and between the orchard rows all the ground was weltering with blue flames of lupin, wild iris, white spottings of popcorn flowers, the yellow of the johnny-jump-ups. Above all, glowing like hot embers, the poppies took whole pasture fields and shone along the margins of the roads and lanes. But all this was only the fire on the ground. Higher up, the plum trees had stopped blooming and offered only translucent clouds of green, but the peach trees were alight with miles and miles of rosy pink that stained the ground and poured out a smoke of perfume on the wind.

It blew in Eagan's face; the flush of the spring went through him like the color through the branches. Carefully he refrained from looking to his left, for there, he knew, he would see the long chasm of Loren's Gulch in which the spring could leave hardly a fingermark of green, for the hydraulic miners in the old days had washed away the soil and left only a dread rubble of boulders and naked walls of rock.

As he pulled up near the front gate of the Martin house, he saw old Henry Martin sitting on the veranda with his hands folded over the top of a walking stick. Winter or summer he was nearly always there in just that position, erect, alert, his hands folded over the knob of his walking stick, looking as if he were about to rise. He was sixty-five, brown as a sailor, and thin, dry, and hard as wood.

Eagan got down from the car, waved to old Martin, and taking the clothesbrush from its wrapping, he brushed himself thoroughly, spending a good deal of time over the cuffs of the trousers. Using the mirror and the comb, he arranged his hair. He took the handkerchief from his breast pocket, shook the dust from it, refolded and returned it to its place. Then he entered the yard.

It was Kate's garden from beginning to

end. No other person ever had planted, weeded, cultivated, pruned, and trained. It was mostly roses; the low, white forehead of the house was crossed and recrossed by the long branches of the climbers and in the beds were groups and clusters of short stalks and bunchy heads. The new sprouts were out, some of them half a foot long and of an almost transparent green, but the younger shoots were as red as hammered copper, and glittered under the sun.

Mr. Martin scorned greetings and farewells alike.

"The sap is running pretty good," said he, as Eagan came through the gate and latched it with proper care behind him.

"Hello, Mr. Martin," said Eagan. "Everything is coming along, all right. Where's Kate?"

"She's gone out," said Martin.

"Where?" said Eagan.

"Oh, out. A lot of places."

His glance held straight before him, not on the street, nor the opposite house, nor the trees beyond it, but toward the curving line of the horizon on the southern hills.

"Where's a lot of places?" suggested Eagan.

"Gone out to the Ripleys."

"I'll go find her there, then."

"She was taking them some duds she made for their little kid. Then she was going on to the Parkers'."

"She can sew," said Eagan. "Kate could make shirts, even, I guess. She can make anything with her hands."

"She can waste a lot of time with her hands," said Martin.

"Waste time?" said Eagan. "What would people do—poor people like the Ripleys—if there wasn't Kate to take care of 'em?"

"They'd put out roots and hold themselves up. Sit down here. You won't find Kate. She had a coupla pies along for I don't know who. Made out of them raspberries that she preserved last summer. I never liked anything better than I liked them raspberries. You remember them raspberries, Jimmy?"

"They were mighty good," agreed Eagan.

He sat down gingerly. Henry Martin's grim, stone-hard face and his far-sighted eyes always disturbed Eagan, but it was plainly a vain chase to follow Kate when she was out distributing charities.

"I was pretty partial to them raspberries," said the old man. "But she took the last big jar. It was two-thirds full. She makes two pies. In the extra big pie plates—the deep ones. She filled those plates full. I smelled it clear out here on the porch. 'Hey, Kate, what are you doing?' I yell. She comes out and shows me the pie plates, filled and frothing with red at the top. I know at one glance. 'That's not for us!' I say. 'Poor dear Mrs. What-not,' says she. Damn poor dear Mrs. What-not, I say. Damn all this trotting around. There's only one cure for the way that she wastes her time."

"She's the finest girl in Tuckerville, or all of Tucker Flat, for that matter. Everybody knows that," pointed out Eagan.

"There's only one thing that would cure her," declared Martin again.

"What might that be?"

"A newspaper," said Martin. "Newspapers are a shortcut across country and no corners to turn and get you to glory just as good and better than a hand-built reputation that depends on gossip."

"I don't understand," said Eagan. "I don't know what you mean."

"I didn't think you would," said Martin. "but you might grow up to it. What keeps my girl laying awake at night and working all day, sewing, cooking, or going out and sitting by a deathbed, and holding the hand of some old fool, or reading aloud, or selling tickets to a charity concert?"

"Because she's good!" said Jim Eagan.

"Because she's ambitious," said Martin. "That's why. A newspaper would save her a lot. Suppose that it printed a picture of her, once in a while, wouldn't the plain eyes of any man tell him that she was pretty? Of course they would. And she'd get a permanent reputation at the same time. 'Charming Leader of Tuckerville's Younger Set Is Charity Patron.' That's the way they write things up. It pretty near poisons a couple dozen of the other girls, and it makes the boys buy new neckties and brush their hats. But unless they's a newspaper to help her out, the harder she works and the more she keeps at it, the more they're gonna take her for granted. Nothing that people get tired of sooner than talking good about others."

"I don't see why that should be," protested Eagan.

"There is only three things that people can say about my girl. She's a nice girl; she's got a good heart; and she treats everybody just the same. Well, they get tired of saying those things. If they can't find something else, they wanta forget about her, and that's what they'll do in spite of the way she works. She's on a treadmill. The faster she runs, the more she stays on the same place. She's made herself into a traveling hospital, grocery store, and dry-goods shop, all free; and now Tuckerville takes her for granted, like the post office or the church. There's no more losing trade than being good. There's nothing that'll make a family or a town or a whole country so damn tired. And I could tell you a story about that: a story about how good Dave Loren was."

"Hold on," said Eagan. "You don't mean the Loren of Loren's Gulch, do you? Why, he killed a man, didn't he?"

"I'm gunna lead up to that," said Martin. "Or maybe you know all about it already?"

He dared Eagan with his eye, shifting it for the first time from the distant horizon. So Eagan shook his head, and Martin again reverted to the sky line.

"Dave Loren," said he, "was the only man among the miners on Tucker Flat that carried a Bible along with his pick. Nobody could get sick without having Dave come along and read a few chapters to him. Nobody could up and die without having Dave turn a few pages over his grave. If there was any lazy thug or crooked gambler that went broke and was starving, Dave would share his last pound of flour with that tramp and treat him to a coupla parables. Nobody could start a fight but Dave would step in between and raise his

255

hand. He made as much trouble in that camp as a damned vigilance committee, and we got pretty tired of him. We used to talk it over now and then, but we couldn't find anything to do about it. And now I wanta tell you what saved that camp from Dave Loren; and what saved Dave Loren from himself."

"What was it?" asked Eagan.

"It was a bottla rum. Dave had gone and got himself a chill doing one of his good works, which was putting splints on a broken leg in a hailstorm. And the man with the broken leg hands him that bottle. Dave never had seen that stuff. 'It's kind of a homemade medicine,' says the man that owned it. Bill Clark was his name. And Dave poured down a good big shot. It tasted cool and watery compared with whisky, but it was full hundred-and-forty proof. Pretty soon it felt like another drink. It was a real repeating, double-action little old bottle, and the first thing you know, Dave had six sizable slugs circulating somewhere inside of him. Then he went off like a rocket laid flat on the ground. You could hear him for miles away.

"We were pretty glad about this. All of us that was near by, we went and shook hands with Bill Clark and finished that bottle for him, and he admitted that it was almost worth a broken leg, what that rum had started; and we told him that it was worth two broken legs.

"In the middle of the racket, bang! goes a gun, and bang! again. And pretty soon we hear that a long-drawn-out mule skinner from Missouri by name of Clyde Way has got it into his mean head to stop Loren from rocketing around, and has gone for him with a gun. But he misses his first shot, and before he can shoot again, Loren takes the gun away from the rat and shoots his head off for him. We gather around. Loren is dead sober and looking sick as he stares down at the leavings of Clyde Way. He has his Bible squeezed to a pulp between his big hands, but it don't occur to him to open it and use it on himself for a comfort.

"He asks us what we want to do with him and when the hanging is to be, and we tell him it will be the next time he starts singing hymns on a Sunday when decent men want to rest around and take it easy. But you couldn't make a joke to Loren. He says that God has put a mark on him and that he's going off by himself, away from the faces of his fellow men, because he's not worthy to enjoy the comfort of their presence.

"So away he goes in the rain and makes his first camp up yonder in the gulch, which was a mighty pretty place in that time. He camps by the creek, and when he starts on the next morning, aiming for nowhere but misery, he sees a little yellow eye winking at him from the pebbles along by the water. Gold, my son. That was how he made his strike. That was his golden day. He forgot the wilderness then. Him and the rest ripped the lining out of Loren's Gulch, and he went back and got himself a house in Boston and a house in New York, and right now he's the grandpa of a railroad and a steel mill.

"But you take a ride up to Loren's Gulch, and by the look of it you'll see what happens when a good man explodes. He always leaves scars! You think over what I'm saying, and while you're thinking, go in the kitchen and fix us up a snack for lunch. Kate won't be back here in time to cook it."

Eagan went to the kitchen. It was so neat that the pattern had been scrubbed from the linoleum on the floor; the stove shone like his own shoes. He felt like an eavesdropper. The sweetness of pastry-baking was still in the air like a secret perfume, and the two window shades were drawn two-thirds of the way down. He never had been able to understand why women darken a room before they leave it, but now as he raised the shades he felt less like a trespasser.

In the pantry, he found cold pork and beans, which he warmed up with fresh slices of bacon in the frying pan. There was coffee also, and bread of Kate's own making, soft, white, and fine of grain. They ate their lunch, finishing on bread and strawberry preserves, Eagan with the appetite of a giant, such as he always had when he sat down at Kate's table. And after lunch they went out and sat through most of the afternoon on the porch, silent a great part of the time.

Eagan had a maddened feeling of the flight of time. The golden day was slipping from him, and when would he find another like it?

"Mr. Martin!" he said suddenly.

"Aye," said the old man.

"I'm gonna ask Kate to marry me. I'm gonna ask her today."

Martin did not even look at him.

"You might of asked her a coupla years back," said he.

"No. There was still a lump of mortgage then."

"Everybody's always tied to a mortgage, one kind or another."

"There's Kate," said Eagan, starting from his chair.

Out of the steep shadow which fell across

the veranda they looked as from the dark mouth of a cave to the brightness of the street, and there in the river of gold was Kate walking with a big young fellow whose face was strange to Eagan.

"Who's that with her?" he asked over his shoulder.

"That's Bud Raymond."

Eagan half turned.

"What's she doing with Raymond?" he asked. "He's not more than two months out of jail."

"Oh, a broken leg, or a busted reputation, it don't matter. Kate's a great patcher."

Eagan turned back to stare uneasily. He laid hold of one of the veranda pillars and his big hand went halfway around it. "But Raymond's no good," said he, muttering, and he almost forgot Kate, so intently did he search the man.

Raymond was as sleek as ever. He had on a dark blue suit that fitted well over the weight of the shoulders and was cut trimly about the narrowing hips. He wore a bow tie and he had on a light gray hat, the brim turning up cavalierly on one side. It never would have occurred to Eagan to wear a hat of that color with a dark suit, but on Raymond it seemed very right. He was set off furthermore by a little white flower in a buttonhole and by a walking stick that flashed like a sword as he walked along, stepping short to keep rhythm with Kate. At the gate they paused.

Kate had her back to the house. She leaned a little against the gate and looked up at Raymond, talking and laughing softly, while he stooped somewhat from his height above her, deprecatory, polite, and genial. He was leaning gracefully, lightly against his walking stick, which he held in his left hand, and in the same hand was a pair of light yellow chamois gloves. Why should gloves be carried, and not worn? thought Eagan. Eagan saw Raymond take off his hat, and, resting his stick on the ground a little before him, he bowed, and sustained his bow, and said something charming in the midst of it.

He was off up the street after that, and Kate calling musically after him a word or two which Eagan did not understand, because in his ears there was a roaring like that of a distant fall of water. She opened the gate, then leaned on it a moment, looking idly up and down the street—chiefly up, no doubt, after the retreating figure of the gallant Raymond. As she turned away, she still was in no hurry to come to the dim forms on the veranda, but paused to lean above a rosebush which was heading out with clusters of small buds.

"The green flies are at them again, Father," said Kate. "The horrible things—we'll have to spray with tobacco and soap again."

Halfway up the path she recognized Eagan, and the recognition stopped her short.

"Jimmy!" she cried. "Why, it's not your regular day! Jimmy, what on earth has happened?"

He went down the steps to meet her and take her hands, but she gave him only one, putting it out in what seemed a gesture of surprise and protest; yet she was so dear to him that, now she was close, he paid no heed to gestures and even could forget the unhappiness which had been aching in his throat the moment before. Into the heart of his chosen day and into his own heart she fitted perfectly with her golden-brown hair and her blue eyes.

"I'll tell you what's happened," he said, climbing the steps beside her. "It's a vacation. You know, after ten years."

"Yes, I know. Sometimes it seems to me a hundred. Poor Jimmy!"

But the sympathy was all in her voice, he thought, and her glance lingered critically about his shoulders. He forced them back with a fresh and more intimate touch of pain that made him say tersely, "Where did you pick him up—Bud Raymond?"

They had come to the top of the steps. She turned and looked at him coldly for a moment before she replied: "I found Bud coming in from the Bradley house. He'd been clear to Bradley Crossing. He walked all the way to see the warehouse people, and what do you think? They wouldn't take him! He told them that he would do anything; he'd work with a hand truck. You know—they always need men: but they told him they were full up. Nobody'll have him. It's a terrible thing—and he keeps so quiet and brave through it all. I don't understand how men can do such things to him!"

"*I* do," said Eagan harshly. "Look what Bud has always been. A loafer. He sponged on his father; he sponged on his brother a couple of years, too, till they kicked him out!"

"It isn't fair. He was a sick man!" cried Kate.

"Oh, come along," said Eagan. "He was always as strong as a horse, though I don't know where he ever got his muscle. He certainly never worked for it. He was never any good, and when he can't sponge off his family, he goes and cracks a safe and gets five years for it."

"You don't know the position he was in,"

said Kate. "It wasn't that he wanted the money for himself, but because—"

"Yeah, Bud was always a great hand at explaining," interrupted Eagan.

"I don't like the way you talk!"

She was breathless with anger.

"I don't like the way that you go around with a yegg like Raymond," he told her.

"I won't kick a poor fellow when he's down."

"You leave him alone," he advised her solemnly. "He's no good. I don't want you to go around with him like that."

She laughed a little. The sound was hard and sharp and stopped suddenly.

"Are you going to tell me what I'm to do?" she demanded. "You have no right!"

"Well," he said, slowly, "it's that right that I've come after. This morning, out at the farm, the hills were like gold, and I thought about you. The land is clean now. There's no mortgage on it, and when I looked around at the morning, I thought about you. I came in to see when you'd marry me."

He waited through the space of three heartbeats.

"I can't," said she.

"Kate," said old Martin, "you run along in and fix some supper. Jimmy, you're a damn fool. Sit down and talk to me."

Neither of them paid the least attention to the old man.

"For ten years," said Eagan, "I've thought that I was walking straight towards you."

"I've always been mighty fond of you, Jimmy," said she.

"You knew what I was working toward. You always knew," he insisted.

"Well, people can change," said she.

"I've not changed. Have *you* changed?" he demanded.

He came a little closer to her, so that his attitude was very like a threat, yet when he saw her stand her ground and tilt up her face, his heart was wrung.

"Yes, I've changed," she said.

"It's Bud Raymond?"

"Yes."

He took off his hat and passed a hand through his hair.

"I guess I'd better be getting along," said he. "Good night."

Neither of them answered, but he went down the path to the gate, fumbled for the latch, missed it, fumbled again, and found it.

"Jimmy!" called the breaking voice of Kate behind him, but he did not want sympathy, so he went out to the Ford and got in. It was not cranked. It made him feel foolish to have to climb out again and start the engine. He saw that she had run halfway down the path and stopped there; then he began the turn which would start him back to the ranch. But he thought of the dampness and the darkness of the farmhouse, and the smell of boiled codfish ineradicably in the corner of the kitchen, so he straightened out the curve with a stagger of the car and went on down the street.

In the center of town he found a vacant place and left the car. He had to go on, he did not know where, for his major dread was that soon he would have to sit quietly, alone with his thoughts.

At the corner of Main Street and Second someone spoke to him. He waved a hand and went on. When he came to the railroad, the gates were shut, so he turned down Front Street, sauntering slowly, and wished that Tuckerville had been larger so that he would have more miles of pavement to walk over.

"Hello, Jimmy," said a voice.

He turned and saw Deputy Sheriff Tom Larkin standing in the middle of the street, a man with a hanging, forward-thrusting head and canny eyes, always alight.

"What're you doing in town this time of day?"

"Seeing the sights," said Eagan. "Any law against that?"

And he walked on.

He put his hands behind his back and locked them hard together.

He passed the front of Bill Meyer's saloon, now a speakeasy. The volume of Bill's business had fallen off since Prohibition, but he was making more money. He had built a new house and supported the charities. Bill had been a slovenly "Dutchman" in the old days, but now he was both neat and eminent.

Eagan knocked at the door and it was opened by a white-jacketed little man with a bald head and a mustache as pale as potato sprouts.

"I don't know you," said he, holding the door.

"You'd better," said Eagan and walked in.

Eagan leaned on the bar with one elbow.

"Gimme a whisky," said he.

Down the bar stood big Bud Raymond with two companions, both rather brightly dressed for Tuckerville.

"Any of you gentlemen know him?" asked the bartender, sweating.

"Sure," answered Raymond. "It's Jimmy Eagan. Hullo, Jimmy, old boy!"

He came forward with a genial smile and

his hand extended, but Eagan stopped him.

"I know you, Raymond," he said. "I know you too damn well. And I don't shake hands with crooks."

Raymond paused, and the hand which had been extended dropped to the edge of the bar.

"You can't get away with that kind of talk," said he.

He looked steadily at Eagan and Eagan looked back silently. He was afraid that if he spoke again the sound would tear his throat.

Raymond turned slowly, his eyes still on Eagan's, and went back to his two companions. They eyed Eagan coldly.

"Easy, boys," said the bartender. "Let's have no trouble."

He drew out the whisky bottle, hesitant, looking wistfully at the new patron. Then, deciding, he thrust it out boldly upon the bar and put a little glass beside it. He even smiled at Eagan when he saw the brown of the hand that grasped the bottle, and the gray calluses which covered the upper side of the forefinger.

"You'll find that pretty good stuff," he said. "What I mean, it's real. That was never cut, that whisky. It's fifty cents a shot. Right up the street here, at Chuck Parmenter's place, it's seventy-five. But I ain't a robber."

He took the half dollar and dropped it into the cash drawer. Eagan poured off the drink.

"It's like water," he said. "Let's have another. It's like water. I can't taste it."

"Well," laughed the bartender, "if you're iron it won't rust you. Here you go!"

Eagan poured again. Again he threw it off. Things were snapping inside him like cords which might bind a giant.

He turned and stared down the bar. He could see the face of big Raymond in the mirror and the faint image of Raymond streaming down the bar. The other seemed to feel the gaze and turned. He smiled: "You wear a skirt, do you?"

"Back up, Bud," said one of his friends. "This is no place. You back up."

Raymond ignored him, staring at Eagan. "I asked you a question—I asked if you wear a skirt."

A growling sound swelled in Jim Eagan's throat as he walked up to Raymond and slapped his face. The flesh was not soft. It was firm and did not seem to give under the stinging tips of his fingers. Then a hand flashed under Eagan's eyes and he was knocked flat on his back. His head struck the footrail of the bar and warm blood ran down his neck.

As he got to his feet again, the bartender

was pleading for order. Raymond was shaking off his two companions.

"I told him I wouldn't take his kind of talk," he said. "I'm going to break his damned neck."

Eagan laughed. He ran in. A blow stopped him. He ran in again. He admired, calmly, the grace and ease of the other as Raymond side-stepped him and clipped him on the jaw with a short punch. The shock of it flung him against the wall; he used the rebound to spring in again, and this time his fist went home. He felt ribs spring under the weight of his knuckles, and striking up with the other hand he reached the head solidly.

Raymond was on his hands and knees, bleeding onto the floor; the bartender's image was waving frantic arms in the mirror; and Raymond's friends, separating, ran in at Eagan from different sides. A bottle flashed like a knife in the hand of one. The other swung a chair, and Eagan tried to get in under the sway of it. He was too late. He felt it crash about his head and shoulders. The face of the man who had wielded it became a white blur, and Eagan struck that blur down to the darkness of the floor.

He turned as the bottle missed his head. His hand fell on the back of another chair, and instantly it was a club in his grasp. The club dwindled, grew lighter. Darkness began to pour through the room, and out of the darkness forms kept looming swiftly at him; there were shocks from behind, from the sides, from in front. Blood ran down into his eyes, and a voice roared and thundered in his ears, following him. It was his own voice.

The window went out. The bar mirror shivered from end to end. He could hear the bartender screaming now, but still the vague forms rushed into the twilight of his mind and he struck them away with the broken fragment of the chair. His knees began to fail. They sagged to the floor, but still he struck out at the shadows before him that rose through the dimness.

Hands that were full of a fresh, new strength mastered him from behind.

"Stop it, Eagan!" shouted a voice in his ear. It was Deputy Tom Larkin. "It's finished, d'you understand? And you've raised sweet hell!"

"Where's Bud Raymond?" asked Eagan. "I can't see him. Show me Bud Raymond."

"His two friends got him into their car, what was left of him, and then they scooted, but we'll have them by tomorrow. We only wanted a charge against them; and now we've got it, they'll have a long rest up the river. This'll close Meyer's place. Maybe you oughta be jailed, but not by me. You've done a good day's work for Tuckerville." He examined Eagan's battered face. "How did the three of them happen to jump you?"

"It was just a little party," said Eagan. "It was only—" The darkness, increasing, rose out of the floor and covered his eyes. . .

He was still in almost utter night when he heard voices, and consciousness came slowly back to him. He was covered from foot to chin in fresh sheets, like the touch of cool water.

Through the shadows of his mind he heard the voice of Larkin saying: "I thought I'd bring him here; I thought he kind of belonged here."

"He does!" cried Kate Martin. "I hope they're sent to prison for life. The cowards, the cowards—"

"Three of 'em, mind you," said Larkin, sounding a note of content like a connoisseur. "And Bud Raymond is no easy thug to handle. It must of been pretty good. They took chairs and bottles to him, but he gives them all the run. He knocked them apart. He must of exploded, kind of, the way that place looked."

Still blinded, Eagan pushed himself to a sitting posture. "I've got to get out of here," said he.

A broad hand was laid on his breast, but he resisted.

"I've got to get out of here. You don't understand, Larkin," said he. "There's only one person has the right to let me stay—"

"Jimmy, my darling!" said Kate.

"You say if it's all right," said Eagan.

"It's going to be all right forever," said she, weeping. "Only if you'll forgive me, it'll be all right."

He allowed himself to be pushed back into the bed.

"We won't be needing you for a bit, I guess," said old Martin.

"No," said Larkin, laughing, "I guess you won't."

Then one of Eagan's eyes opened a little, painfully, so that he could see the white of the ceiling; from the other eye he would be able to see nothing for many a day. But as his eye widened and he could see the stain of the sunset spreading over the ceiling, in the same manner his stunned brain took in more and more the meaning of the girl's words until at last it was like the casting open of a door in a dark room; a whole beautiful world

273

rushed in upon him.

"Father," said she, "you watch him. Watch him very closely. I have to get some more iodine. Don't take your eyes off him one second, because he's not himself yet."

"A drunk that goes out and wrecks a saloon and gets himself beat up," said Mr. Martin. "I dunno that I'd bother so much about him."

"Father," said she, in anger, "how dare you say such a thing?"

"Ah," said the old man, "You could see it for yourself, and smell it on his breath!"

"The most honest, gentle, good, quiet—and he goes to throw himself away for me—I'm a detestable creature, and he'll never forgive me—and I'll never forgive myself—"

Her voice trailed away into the distance through the house as she hurried for the medicine.

"Mr. Martin," said Eagan, "d'you think that Kate has really changed her mind? Does she *care* for me?"

"If you'd heard some of the row that she's been making over you," said Martin, "you wouldn't need an interpreter. I think she *does* care, all of a sudden. Women are that way; changeable. I'm might sorry for you, Jimmy."

"I'm gunna be all right," said Eagan. "I'm practically all right now."

"That's what you think," said Martin, "because no young fool can look on the hind side of a wedding day. But the time'll come when you'll find out that every week has seven mornings, and only one of them is Sunday and out on a farm there ain't even a Sunday to speak of. But why I'm mostly sorry for you is the kind of a start you've made. It's the pace that kills, Jimmy, and a slow start is what you want for a long race."

"I don't know what you mean by all that," said Eagan.

"Ain't it plain that Kate is a nacheral patcher? I couldn't keep her busy at home. Can you?"

"I don't understand," said Eagan.

"You wait and just grow, and one day you'll reach the idea without even standing on tiptoe," said Martin.

But thought was still difficult for Eagan. He preferred to listen to the light and hurried footfall of Kate, returning down the hall.

The publishers hope that this
Large Print Book has brought
you pleasurable reading.
Each title is designed to make
the text as easy to see as possible.
G. K. Hall Large Print Books are
available from your library and
your local bookstore. Or you can
receive information on upcoming
and current Large Print Books by
mail and order directly from the
publisher. Just send your name
and address to:

G. K. Hall & Co.
70 Lincoln Street
Boston, Mass. 02111

or call, toll-free:

1-800-343-2806

A note on the text
Large print edition designed by
Bernadette Montalvo.
Composed in 18 pt Plantin
on a Mergenthaler 202
by Compset Inc., Beverly MA.

FL 186877 L

Brand
Max Brand's best western stories,
Vol. II

DATE DUE			
OCT 4 1995			
MAY 9 1996			
JUL 1 5 1996			